PRAIRIES
OF
FEVER

D1605855

PRAIRIES
OF
FEVER

A Novel by
Ibrahim Nasrallah

translated from the Arabic by
May Jayyusi and Jeremy Reed

introduction by
Fedwa Malti-Douglas

INTERLINK BOOKS

An imprint of Interlink Publishing Group, Inc.

NEW YORK

First published in English 1993 by

INTERLINK BOOKS
An imprint of Interlink Publishing Group, Inc.
99 Seventh Avenue
Brooklyn, New York 11215

Originally published in Arabic as
Barāri 'l-Hummā by Mu'assasat al-Abhāth al-'Arabiyya,
and Dār al-Shurūq, Beirut, 1985

Library of Congress Cataloging-in-Publication Data

Naṣr Allāh, Ibrāhīm.
    [Barārī al-ḥummá. English]
    Prairies of fever / a novel by Ibrahim Nasrallah; translated from
the Arabic by May Jayyusi and Jeremy Reed; introduction by Fedwa
Malti-Douglas.
        p.   cm. — (Emerging voices)
    Translation of: Barārī al-ḥummá.
    ISBN 1–56656–103–5 — ISBN 1–56656–106–X (pbk.)
    I. Title. II. Series.
PJ7852.A688B3713 1993
892'.736—dc20   92–23386
                                                            CIP

Cover painting by Ahmad Nawash, courtesy of The Royal Society
of Fine Art, Jordan National Gallery of Fine Art, Amman, Jordan.

Printed and bound in the United States of America

10   9   8   7   6   5   4   3   2   1

PRAIRIES
OF
FEVER

This translation was prepared by PROTA, Project of Translation from Arabic Literature, founded and directed by Salma Khadra Jayyusi.

Other PROTA titles in print:

The Secret Life of Saeed, the Ill-Fated Pessoptimist, a novel by Emile Habiby. Trans. by S. K. Jayyusi and Trevor LeGassick. 1982; 2nd ed. 1985.

Wild Thorns, a novel by Sahar Khalifeh. Trans. by Trevor LeGassick and Elizabeth Fernea. 1985 and 1989.

Songs of Life, poetry by Abu 'l-Qasim al-Shabbi. Trans. by Lena Jayyusi and Naomi Shihab Nye. 1985.

War in the Land of Egypt, a novel by Yusuf al-Qa'id. Trans. by Olive Kenny and Christopher Tingley. 1986.

Modern Arabic Poetry: An Anthology. 1988 and 1991.

The Literature of Modern Arabia: An Anthology. 1987 and 1991.

All That's Left to You, a novella and collection of short stories by Ghassan Kanafani. Trans. by May Jayyusi and Jeremy Reed. 1990.

A Mountainous Journey, an autobiography by Fadwa Tuqan. Trans. by Olive Kenny. 1990.

The Sheltered Quarter, a novel by Hamza Bogary. Trans. by Olive Kenny and Jeremy Reed. 1991.

The Fan of Swords, poetry by Muhammad al-Maghut. Trans. by May Jayyusi and Naomi Shihab Nye. 1991.

A Balcony Over the Fakihani, a collection of three novellas by Liyana Badr. Trans. by Peter Clark with Christopher Tingley. 1993.

Legacy of Muslim Spain. Essays on Islamic Civilization in the Iberian Peninsula. Ed. Salma Khadra Jayyusi. 1992.

Anthology of Modern Palestinian Literature. 1992.

Acknowledgements

I should like to thank the author, Ibrahim Nasrallah, for his help in facilitating the preparation of this work in its English translation, and for promptly and graciously answering my many questions. My thanks also go to the translators, May Jayyusi and Jeremy Reed, for their deep interest in this novel, and for their labor of love in rendering this work into English.

PROTA also gratefully acknowledges the support of Dr. Ghada Hijjawi Qaddumi in this project, as well as Dr. Fedwa Malti-Douglas for her introduction.

Salma Khadra Jayyusi

Glossary

Abu   Father of. Parents are usually called
                       by the name of their first born male
                       child: thus the father of a first born
                       male child called Muhammad is
                       Abu Muhammad, and his mother is
                       called Um Muhammad. If no male
                       child is born, the parents may be
                       called by the name of their first born
                       daughter.

Amm   Paternal uncle; any older man who
                       should be addressed respectfully.

Dashdash   Flowing gowns worn by men in the
                       Gulf countries.

Mulukhiyya   A vegetable dish made of the green
                       leaves of the *mulukhiyya* plant,

	cooked usually with meat or chicken.
Mutawwi	A man commissioned to make the rounds at prayer times (five during the day) and see that all men went to prayer. He can be quite threatening at times.
al-Qunfudhah	A little town in southern Saudi Arabia.
Riyal	The Saudi monetary unit.
Shaikh	Usually, an old man. The word is used as a title of great dignity by the upper echelons of the ruling class in the Gulf area, including rulers.
Umm	Mother. See note under Abu.
Ustadh	Master; learned man; teacher (as in this novel); university professor.

Translator's Foreword

Ibrahim Nasrallah's *Prairies of Fever* is the Arabic answer to the divided self, that image of the double or shadow of which Jung took account, and which surfaces in the European novel from Dostoyevsky to Herman Hesse's *Steppenwolf,* and from Thomas Mann's *Death in Venice* to Jean-Paul Sartre's *Nausea,* and wherever the inner dialogue in its psychic expression is realized as a discourse between two: I and another, the mirror and its reflection.

Prairies of Fever is remarkable for its preoccupation with duality—Muhammad Hammad and his double who answers to the same name and description achieve a dialogue through the tension of irreconcilables—the living and the dead. The protagonist of the book is pronounced dead at the opening, he must pay for his own burial, and yet somehow there has been a mistake. He is alive; but the double who shares his life has gone missing, and it is the search for the other which comprises the psychodynamic obsession of this disturbing novel.

Nasrallah's objective has by its very nature to remain unresolved, but what we are given by way of its enquiry has all the hallucinatory intensity of a prose-poem, an uncompromising, conflagratory lyric that is not without that particular humor of the absurd which marks the encounter between the irrational and situations which provoke its correspondingly extreme behavior. Nasrallah has written a novel in which the experiential I is without any stable pivot of rest. The result is a dynamited vulner-ability, an apprehension of the desert through a con-sciousness whose antennae create and interpret fear. In the face of overwhelming crises, Muhammad Hammad does not so much retreat as transform his reading of the event into something so terrible that the fear is annihi-lated. This is the reverse of blacking out when confronted by terror; it is more a reckless desire to magnify the unconfrontable into a force that destroys itself by exceed-ing the boundaries of containment.

A man in the desert, a teacher at al-Qunfudhah, is woken up by the police who demand payment for having buried him. He is a man of diminished proportions— everything outside and around him is unremittingly vast—the intractable desert, the mountains, the distance between villages. His way of increasing his stature is to admit to the companionship of another. Lacking help, he has to believe in the autonomous existence of someone who shares his name, his characteristics, his occupation and the bat-infested room in which he lives. This other becomes his motivating force—the narrative quest in pursuit of the other naturally intersects with a community who still lives by the laws of the desert. Saad's daughter disappears and becomes a voice in the wilderness, Ahmad Lufti turns into a wolf who hunts with the pack, the metamorphic stage is always an open possibility—people supersede their own dimensions and break out to inhabit another variant incarnation. The primal is a powerful force, it is the chaos that preceded language, roads, civilization, and anyhow, as the narrator says, "we had already smashed the English language out of recognition." And once nominalism and the ordering principles of language have disappeared, we are back to the apprehension of the world through the animated imagination. All of Nasrallah's characters are one character for they are all interchangeable. The desert, he says, eliminates gender: they are somehow neither man nor woman, they are inchoate, on the edge of becoming, or open to invasion by other, stronger sensibilities. Illusion and reality, identity and amnesia, these are the polar opposites which attract in *Prairies of Fever* and assume a transshifting fluidity in the course of events.

This is a novel in which any transformation is possible due to its being a satellite of the one instructing imaginative beam—the narrator's hallucinative inner eye. Nasrallah has reintroduced the protean theme of metamorphosis to the novel: his is a mind capable of erecting sky-pyramids or unleashing a torrential spring from a rock-face. His journey has been through fire and one might say his words singe the paper; they reach always for what is most important in art, the transformational process whereby inner and outer worlds lose their distinction, and the two fuse in the dynamics of metaphor.

Prairies of Fever is about extremes. It should be read for its fearless vision, its concern with the mind in isolation, and for its absolute trust that poetry alters the world. It is right that such a novel takes place in the desert—Nasrallah has given us a black sun risen above white sands—a new constellation of inner space.

Jeremy Reed

Introduction

In this extraordinary novel, published in Arabic in 1985, Ibrahim Nasrallah joins the growing ranks of postmodern Arabic authors. If the postmodern sensibility is marked by a sense of rupture, of loss, or of absolute unredeemable exile, then few authors have been better prepared for it by the circumstances of their lives than Ibrahim Nasrallah. For his is a story of exile within exile. Born in 1954 in the Wahdat Palestinian refugee camp in Jordan's capital city Amman, Nasrallah studied at the Teachers Training College in Amman and then went to work as a teacher in Saudi Arabia. He is now back in Jordan, where he devotes his time to journalism and writing. Ibrahim Nasrallah has made his mark on Arabic literature predominantly through his poetry. His numerous volumes of verse include *Horses at the Outskirts of the*

1

City (1980), *The Rains Inside* (1982), and, most recently, *The Youth River and the General* (1987). Nasrallah has also turned his pen to children's poetry. *Prairies of Fever* is his first novel.

The Arabic novel, less than a century old, has already experienced many transformations. For at least the last decade, and probably for the first time in its history, Arabic narrative is evolving in parallel with developments conditioning this prose genre throughout the world. From the *nouveau roman*, with its disintegration of traditional narrative assumptions, to the most recent postmodernist experiments, Arabic prose literature has more than kept abreast, it has made an important (though too often ignored) contribution. And Arabic writers have done so through their own culturally distinctive literary innovations.

What is the postmodern impulse in Arabic fiction? Certainly, it is difficult to encompass this highly significant complex of narrative developments within a few lines. Perhaps most striking has been the exploitation of what has been referred to in the West as metafiction or self-conscious narrative: a heightened awareness of the narrative process, involving (among other techniques) the intrusions of a self-conscious narrator or making the act of writing (or its absence) the center of the text itself. The novels of Yusuf al-Qa'id have adapted these practices to a distinctive vision of Egyptian society.

Also characteristic of Arabic postmodernism (and far more important than similar developments in the West) is a process of writing through (or rewriting) the distinctive discourse of classical Arabic literature, effectively redefining that literature and the traditional culture which nurtured it.

Jamal al-Ghaytani has become famous for his neo-Mamluk and other medieval fictions. Traditional fragments form part of the revolutionary narrative explorations of the Palestinian Emile Habiby. Less well known, but equally brilliant, are the comic, playful destructions of traditional story-telling discourse served over a bed of philological allusions by Muhammad Mustajab.

That Ibrahim Nasrallah's novel partakes of this trend is, thus, not surprising. Unique in Nasrallah's venture, however, but explicable given his background, is the intense poetic presence in the novel. It is not just that poetry abounds; the language of the prose itself is so metaphorical, so rich in allusions and images that it seems at times to read like verse.

Prairies of Fever revolves around a teacher in a village in a remote area of Saudi Arabia, al-Qunfudhah. His interactions with the local inhabitants form the background of the story. This is a traditional enough subject. The adventures of a teacher in a remote village have been chosen by a number of Middle Eastern authors: the Iranian Jalal Al-e Ahmad in *The School Principal*, the Syrian 'Abd as-Salam al-'Ujayli in "The Dream," the Egyptian Yusuf al-Qa'id in *The Days of Drought*, to name but three. Such a setting permits the elaboration of a number of issues dear to many Arab (and other third world) authors: the clash of East and West, of traditional and modern, of individual and bureaucracy. Like al-Qa'id, however, Nasrallah has tended to avoid these now hackneyed civilizational themes. Most often, of course, the inspiration for the narrative is also a personal one, the writer having indeed taught in an isolated area. This is as true of Nasrallah as it is of al-Qa'id. Hence, it is not so

3

much the subject of *Prairies of Fever* which draws our attention but the manner in which it is woven into a narrative.

In a discussion of the novel's background, Nasrallah poetically writes of his experience in the area of al-Qunfudhah, a region whose center is the city of the same name situated on the Red Sea, approximately four hundred miles south of Jedda, and in which "life is below zero": "I caught malaria more than once and the disease almost took my life. I believe that I lived an experience close to death, rather I touched its edges . . . Malaria is native there, as are monkeys and tigers. Vipers are lavishly abundant, as are spiders and white ants, as well as harsh exile (*ghurba*)."* The highly charged term, *ghurba*, expresses an emotional as well as physical separation from one's homeland. A powerful experience, indeed, for Ibrahim Nasrallah, the poet, for whom the writing of this novel was no easy task. In an interview in *al-Maghrib al-'Arabi*, the author explained that the attempt to set down *Prairies of Fever* extended from 1977 to 1983, involving many painful writings and rewritings.

The opening incident in the novel depicts a first person narrator, the school teacher, who is asked by five intruders to pay for his own funeral. And this, much against his protestations that he is indeed alive. But as the story progresses, the question is raised: is it this first person narrator or is it his roommate who has disappeared, and about whom the fuss is being made? This sets in motion an intricate, if not nightmarish, game of identity and loss of self.

* The details on the novel are provided in a personal document written by the author and addressed to Dr. Salma Khadra Jayyusi, Director of PROTA, and which she has kindly made available to me.

When questioned by an official, the hero reveals that his roommate was stricken by fever and was asked to pay for his own funeral. The identity of this roommate is problematic from his first appearance in the text: the hero calls him his "colleague," while the police refer to him as his "friend." The elusive individual's name is Muhammad Hammad, oddly enough the name of the hero as well. Asked why both bear the same name, the hero answers: "I do not know. It is surely a coincidence." Coincidences in this narrative, however, seem to abound: the physical description the hero Muhammad provides of his colleague Muhammad is identical to his own.

Names are, of course, the essence of the identity of any individual. And, in a literary work, appellations are extremely significant. In postmodern fiction, in which the world can become a topsy-turvy place, this is all the more the case. How interesting it then becomes to have the two identically named characters bearing the appellation Muhammad Hammad. Both words are derived from the same Arabic verbal root, *h-m-d*, and both are related to the idea of praise. Hamada (without the doubled "m") is also the nickname for one who is named Muhammad. In a sense, both partners in this onomastic system, Muhammad and Hammad, revolve linguistically around one another, are enmeshed one in the other. The two identical appellations are, thus, themselves composed of two virtually interchangeable parts. It should not surprise us then that Muhammad should be told that he looks as though he lost half of himself.

This confusion of identity on the level of the plot is reinforced by the highly original and unique exploitation of narrative voice. In fact, it is probably the system of narration that most clearly places *Prairies of Fever* within the postmodern domain. The first element the reader encounters is a break in narration, a change in the narrative voice, at the beginning of the second chapter. Changes in narrative voice are not unusual in modern Arabic literature. One can find them, for example, as early as the 1920s in Taha Husayn's autobiography, *al-Ayyam*, in which a third-person narration features intrusions by a first-person one. What is revolutionary in Nasrallah's case is that the initial first-person narration is broken by second person narration. It is a "you" (i.e. "you did this," "you did that") with whom the reader must become familiar, as opposed to the "I" or, of course, to the traditional story-telling of a third-person narrator.

Second-person narration, that is a consistent exploitation of the "you" and not simply a narrator (be it first or third person) addressing an individual in the second person, is apparently unique in modern Arabic literature, and relatively rare in world literature. Michel Butor wove an entire narrative in the second person, *La modification*, a literary experiment of great ambition and success. Butor's text, however, shows consistent narration, that seemingly objective third-person narrator being absent from it. And the narration of an entire text in one voice, no matter which, creates a mood, enveloping the narrative. This certainly is the case for *La modification*.

Prairies of Fever draws an entirely different narrative map. After the title, the text opens with almost a full page of poetry, something to which we shall return below. What is significant here is that this poetry is presented by a third-person narrator. Then follows the initial prose chapter, opened by a first-person narrator, the one asked

6

to pay for his funeral. This is succeeded by that second-person narration, mentioned above. Hence, three possible narrative situations with their attendant voices are created within the first few pages of the text.

And these three narrative voices continue throughout *Prairies of Fever*, helping to create a sort of unreality in which the characters and their actions are bathed. The reader is torn between the supposedly objective and impersonal narrator of the opening lines who sets up a rough picture of the background against which the story will unfold (yet the "objective" voice is in verse, hence "poetic") and the two other voices which seem strangely interlaced. The pervasive nature of the second-person narrator functions as a type of control over the character being addressed, Muhammad Hammad. When the latter, however, manages to speak in the first-person, it is as though he breaks away from this narrative constraint to regain his own first-person voice, his autonomy. Is it an accident that this narrative taking-of-possession by the first-person is most often related to the questions of identification between the two individuals named Muhammad Hammad?

This fragmentation on the level of the narrators is reinforced by a fragmentation in the forms of the narrative itself. *Prairies of Fever* includes within it a great deal of poetry, perhaps to be expected given the author's experience with that literary form. More unusual is the insertion at a certain point of the external signs of a play. The reader is presented with a "scene" and a "curtain." Such devices, of course, are standard postmodern fare, but with Nasrallah, these elements lead to a unique literary vision. His is a fantastic, oneiric, occasionally nightmarish world created not only by the diversity of narrative voices and the loss of identity but also by a range of other literary techniques. Perhaps the most powerful in this context is anthropomorphization. The very environment and objects surrounding the central character come alive. The road being built becomes a giant black being, the village, a fever-infested "lung of the desert." The second-person narrator advises: "No. Don't be sad over the fact that the table will not share with you after today a can of sardines, or a can of chick peas, or a loaf of bread. No. Don't be sad." This poignantly ironic anthropomorphization evokes the sharing of meals, a sacred activity in Arab culture, and the loneliness and alienation of canned foods.

This example also calls attention to a favored technique in Nasrallah's text, repetition. This type of repetition has a long history in Arabic narrative, going back to the Qur'an. Here, however, this procedure is combined with that of anthropomorphization and it reinforces part of the statement, as with the stylistically similar repetitions of Taha Husayn's classic autobiography.

But the oneiric in *Prairies of Fever* permits the creation of another type of repetition, one imbued with ambiguity and uncertainty:

That morning Ustadh Muhammad came.
"What morning?"
"I don't know."
That morning, but it wasn't exactly morning, it was noon. That noon
"What noon?"
"I don't know."
That noon, but it wasn't exactly noon, it was evening.
"What evening?"

8

"I don't know."

That evening, but it wasn't exactly evening . . . that . . .

"I don't know."

This environment in which the narrative is set, these "prairies of fever," seem to be conducive to the creation of ambiguities, to the elimination of individuality. After all, the text tells us that even the difference between the sexes disappears in the desert.

These specific ambiguities extend to a larger domain of uncertainty, in a manner reminiscent of both the *nouveau roman* and many postmodern texts. Exactly what transpires is sometimes open to question. When one of the characters disappears, variant interpretations are given: some said he was eaten by wolves, whereas shepherds claimed that they saw him roaming among the packs of wolves. Variants are an integral part of classical Arabic narrative, whether sacred (as in the *hadith*, the sayings and actions of the Prophet) or secular (*adab*, anecdotal texts, biographies, for example). Hence, the variants in *Prairies of Fever* constitute an evocation of classical forms typical of Arab postmodern writing, just as they call attention to the narrative process and underline the uncertainty of events.

But this exploitation of the traditional in Nasrallah's narrative is minimal, in comparison with many other contemporary Arab authors. The virtual absence of tradition in the oneiric world of Muhammad Hammad separates this fantastic universe from any tangible other world, rendering the text, in a sense, more insular, more desperate, and more absurd. The conversation Muhammad has with the five individuals who want him to pay for his own funeral so that it can befit someone like him is a case in point. He asks them if he is dead, to which they answer in the affirmative. Then he asks them again if they want the money from him, to which they again answer in the affirmative. He then asks them if they will leave him alone so that he will never see them again. They reply: "You will never see us. How will you see us, O lunatic, since you are dead, how?"

Nasrallah's use of the absurd differs, thus, from that of that other Palestinian author, Emile Habiby. With the latter, despite the fantastic plots, the dazzling word-games, and the daring combinations of literary forms, one retains a modicum of order through the exploitation of the classical tradition: something tangible, something from another literary reality, seemingly outside, but of course really within, the text. Fragmented, out of place, Habiby's classical evocations function as a distant, even nostalgic echo of an ideal order. *Prairies of Fever*, through its separation from the classical literary world (present only in a principle of ambiguity, the variant), deepens a typically Arab postmodern malaise. More radically absurd than that of Habiby, more intimate than that of Yusuf al-Qa'id, Nasrallah's vision questions the identity, even the existence, of the individual as social reality and conscious subject.

Fedwa Malti-Douglas
Indiana University

10

1

Southward, southward
where the Red Sea is
and the white sharks
and al-Qunfudhah
Southward, southward
where sticky swarms of flies
blacken the coffee-bar tables
and the city's main streets
terminate in the void
and the waters rushing from the heights of Aseer
project themselves in vain toward the blue
Southward, southward
men poured down from the north
or flew back to it
and the only harvest that ravaged them
was a murderous isolation
an accelerated anguish.

There were five of them. This is the only fact. Five, without features. The darkness was pitch black and the space around us created a void. The desert crawled in the direction of the threshold. The threshold gripped its own stones and my feet in a last attempt to remain in a circle of green vegetation.

What had happened? In the confusion they told me I'd died, and that I had to pay a thousand *riyals* as a contribution to my funeral expenses. It was then I realized a conspiracy was being enacted against me.

With one collective voice they informed me, without giving me the chance to locate my words, that death didn't exempt me from payment, and that all the other teachers in this sector of the desert had agreed to pay their burial costs.

The circle closed in on me. "Throughout our rounds tonight, we've encountered no one with your morose features, nor have we heard a single word of protest."

The ring tightened. Trying to keep myself together, I managed to say, "This is a silly move. Do you really think you can deceive an intelligent man like me?"

And they laughed!

I thought quickly, trying for the easiest way to regain my composure. Without letting them see, I felt my pulse, then let my fingers travel up to my chest. Everything appeared normal, my heart was regular and my veins echoed its beats. I don't know what brought Haj Abu Azmi's mill to my imagination at that moment, or more correctly to my ear drums:

Bum, bum, bum, bum.

This rhythmic coursing of my blood was the one proof I needed. I waved my arms joyfully in their faces.

"My heart is still beating," I said.

With one voice they replied: "That's no proof you're alive."

I checked my memory to assure myself it was still functioning. And in order to be doubly sure I went deeper until I arrived at that mischievous swelling at the bottom. This particular symbol has its own narrative, and the only clue I'll offer you is to say that it represents a strain of laughter. In order not to increase your perplexity, I'll tell you it's the ringing laughter of my little brother, Nu'man.

I lifted my hand so I could feel the breath exhaled and inhaled by my nostrils. At that moment, I would have liked to breathe out of every pore of my body, but the conspiracy had me retract in the interest of dignity, balance and the preservation of strength. Any trace of weakness would leave me a prey to them.

Laughing—and usually this laugh which fluctuates between tears and indifference afflicts me—I said, "How can I be dead and speak to you at the same time?"

My eyes frantically tried to follow my features as I spun around myself. For an instant I was sure I'd outwitted them with my argument. But there again, I had no assurance of that. The night was impenetrably black, and nothing stood between the courtyard of the house and the desert but a single hut shaped like a clown's hat.

Their heads moved and they faced each other. Their voices expressed surprise when they said, "The man doesn't believe us!" Then they proceeded to swear the most sacred oaths that I'd died just before sunset.

"The crux of the matter is that you're stingy, and don't want to part with a thousand *riyals*. Why don't you be honest about it?"

"You can't deceive me," I said.

When they dispersed, they shouted back at me with one voice:

"We'll go on collecting donations to bury you." This is a procedure that comes into force whenever the desert swallows a teacher.

I was about to tell them I could release them from this task, when they disappeared. They'd come from the night and returned to it.

Of course I was frightened.

At the powerful roar of their motorbikes, and the flood of their headlights, foxes darted into cover. My white hen, crouched on a dry branch that protruded out of the wall and extended into the darkness over the top of the door, fidgeted. The cock searched the light, but didn't crow. As far as I could see my black hen remained motionless.

No sooner had they gone than I realized my vulnerability. I was naked, except for my fear, and exposed to the eye of the infinite. I began to mourn my own death, and to feel terrified that news of it should reach my brother, Nu'man, despite my antagonism to his mischievous laugh. And between two blinding tears I asked myself, "What will my mother do?"

2

Although the sea's distant, a cool wave swings on the tip of your nose, then subsides silently, leaving in its wake a subdued echo. A cool wave that oscillates, then breaks in a dazzling drizzle on your face: air, air, air, air.

In one decisive movement you wipe your nostrils, and your fingers return, charged with live embers.

One night summarizes a lifetime's boredom. It collects it in one body, before it scatters it. One single night.

One night between twilight and daybreak.

One night. But the wave crawls, quivers, and your cells are dispersed across the walls. It spins like disorbited stars, then crashes again at the contours of your bones, gathering itself.

Everything you remember, and everything that's lost to memory, hits in at your skull with black wings and sharp talons. They wheel up into the sky, only to return.

A bright light showed, as though emitted from a strange dream. You opened your eyes. Yes, you could do that. You sat up in bed. Everything weighed: your head, your hand, your fingers, the shadows and the light.

As your head dropped with fatigue, you threw a glance at the opposite bed, the other iron bed on the opposite side of the room, and a violent shock rocked you:

A man can't be horizontal and have four equal sides.

That's how he looked as he lay motionless in the bed.

In the fire-burst of the moment, crowded with emotions, questions and imaginings, you took the cover off your body and, in the distance you crossed, separating the two beds, it seemed as if you were running across a desert.

The hot sand scratches at your feet in a sharp glitter, and the distance keeps on stretching in front of you, as if you were running while standing still.

Your fingers held on to the cover. You didn't hesitate, not that there was room for indecision, and the tension was like a time-bomb about to explode. Everything narrowed, and you felt as though you'd been squeezed in a stone room at the end of the world.

The cover flew off and spread itself over the sacks of white corn behind your bed.

You were assailed by one terrible question. "Where had he gone?"

His briefcase had settled in the middle of the bed . . . a black receptacle with one of its corners swollen with papers, ever since that day you spent in the trunk of a jeep packed with ice, traveling between Jedda and al-Qunfudhah, through a long dusty night.

I said, "This is a childish move, and unconvincing. If he has to take flight, there's no need for him to slip away like this, leaving his briefcase on the bed."

You glanced towards the table and saw his green residence card lying there.

You thought, "He can't go anywhere without that document."

You had, the night before, overheard a little of the conversation that took place at the door to the room. You might have thought you were dreaming, when you said, "If there's a problem, he'll solve it."

"It's true then!"

You turned over the bed cover, the pillow, then your hand stretched to make contact with the clothes inside the briefcase . . . got a firm hold on what it found . . . pulled out a number in confusion, scattering banknotes . . . one hundred, two . . . a thousand . . . You felt happy, you couldn't believe your luck, as you realized he hadn't paid yet!

Yesterday he had told you he had a thousand *riyals* left, the remainder of his April salary.

You checked your brow for fever, and felt a temperature, a cold sweat. You tried to focus through the flaming spears that stuck in your mind, and redirect your thoughts.

"He may have been kidnapped, or killed!" you said.

Then you remembered Fatima. You hardly dared envisage the anguish she'd undergo when she came to know about the death of her bird.

Sweat increased on your forehead, and dripped on to the lower part of your neck. Your eyes filled with terror, and inscrutable questions.

17

You saw the door, the iron door of the room, as though you'd just discovered its presence by chance, you, who are always looking even for the smallest window.

You ran towards the door, to be confronted by the expanse of the desert, consecutive sandhills, impenetrable to sight, now barred the way between your footsteps and the threshold. You turned the key and jumped over the large white stone that forbiddingly guarded your room. You looked at the horizon with its curious mixture of night and day, its cycle of life and death. And like a fisherman on the open sea, you scanned the emptiness, searching for a movement, a sign of life, a hint of green.

Nothing on that blank skyline indicated the presence of a world in motion. Al-Qunfudhah stood alone, with its barren mountains, and its cracked stony hide. It was like carrion scavenged by wolves, foxes, hyenas and snakes, a place eroded by bitter nights.

My watch-hand completed its circle to show the time at eight o' clock. The low fireball of the sun appeared to be climbing the mountain. The room was still in shadow, for the mountain's high. It takes another half an hour for the sun to arrive, and when it does we're exposed to the blazing incandescence of the May noons.

You took a few more steps towards the threshold. Little Mu'ida alone was filling the silence with her screams and the bleating of her sheep. You took off your pajamas. Mu'ida had stopped there, in front of the door, and through the wide open window you saw her run off, emitting the same screams, as if nothing had happened.

As you put on your pants, it struck you it would be better to wear the *dashdash*. That way you'd win the confidence of the head of police.

There was no way of avoiding crossing the land that went towards the precinct at Sabt Shimran. You knew too, that the disappearance of a human being is no trivial matter, and an issue like this would see you in the hands of the executioner in no time at all.

You took the precaution of nudging your memory, so you'd be ready to give decisive answers, which would leave no room for doubt. But anyway, why should they be suspicious when confronted by the truth?

You continued to wonder how he could just disappear, leaving no word, no clue that could help you in establishing his whereabouts. You tried once again to recollect what you'd heard at the door last night, but you couldn't guess what had happened after they'd asked for the thousand *riyals*.

Did he arouse their anger, and as a consequence was kidnapped? Perhaps, but they were mad to come to a man who was alive and ask him to participate in the costs of his own funeral. Or had he fled, or been divided among them and taken to the nearest neighborhood cemetery?

These were possibilities you turned over in your mind as you came down the little dune that lies half way between Thuraiban and Sabt Shimran, before climbing the other stony hill in the direction of the cemetery.

You were like someone about to commit a crime. You roamed among the graves, careful not to step on any of them. There were no signs of a freshly dug grave. You paced the boundaries of the small graveyard, its constrictions amplifying the presence of the dead.

You thought, "Perhaps they've taken him to Sabt Shimran. There the graveyard's larger, and it has a mud wall that fortifies it and preserves its sanctity from inroads by the rabble—although it's a favorite place of ravens, too."

You stood there at the beginning of things. You looked around. Sabt Shimran looked almost empty, and the graveyard lay silent and deserted on the southern side of the village.

This was a large cemetery for a small village like Sabt Shimran. It was like a city, a metropolis that had swallowed scores of villages in the centuries that had passed over this one village.

You felt your heart contract at the thought that graveyards outgrow the local inhabitants.

Damp mounds of earth, still unscorched by the sun, were indications of freshly dug graves. You approached, but they were all graves without names. Wide villages without gravestones.

You thought of going to Fatima, but changed your mind. You prepared yourself for the inevitable crossing between the cemetery and the police precinct. How could truth be ascertained in this no-man's-land?

You climbed the stone steps heavily—three miles dragged their distance under the exposure of the flaming May sun. At last, the precinct stretched in front of you.

You shouted your greetings.

No one answered.

An officer, who's the head of the precinct, and two policemen. Four naked walls; an aura of boredom and viscosity. Here time revolves between ash flicked into the air and the dormant sitting on long wooden seats like those in cafes.

The officer looked at you as though you didn't exist.

20

One of the policemen scratched his leg robustly, and the third turned his head to the wall.

You sat down.

You knew in advance it would take time. After a few minutes you lost hope anyone would ask you anything, so you said: "I woke up today, and there was no trace of my roommate. All I found was his briefcase on the bed."

The officer turned his head to the wall, and said, "And then?"

You said, "Yesterday he was sick. He was feverish in the afternoon. His condition wasn't cause for undue alarm until they came after midnight and asked him to pay one thousand *riyals* towards his funeral expenses; but he refused. I discovered this today when I counted his money. Imagine, they wanted him to pay for his own burial. This morning he was gone."

"Who were these men?"

"I don't know. I only heard their voices."

"What's your roommate's name?"

You couldn't discern who was questioning you, whether it was the officer or one of the two policemen. Two faces outlined against the wall, and a voice steeped in lethargy.

"His name is Muhammad Hammad."

The head of the precinct fidgeted slightly in his wooden chair, and waved his two naked feet with their wiry hairs. Then he placed his right foot on the floor.

"And what's your name?"

Already you'd realized the impossibility of being comprehended. You were shaking all over like a leaf about to separate from its branch and fall.

You said, "Muhammad Hammad."

21

The duplication went unnoticed, and the officer continued his questions:

"You're a stranger to Sabt Shimran, aren't you?"

Before you had time to answer, one of the policemen, the one who'd scratched his leg, approached his chief and whispered something. "Oh, I see!" the chief answered, and turning to you, he said: "But tell me, how do you two have the same name?"

"I don't know. It must be a coincidence, Sir."

You cursed yourself inside for saying that. It was shameful for a man like you to address the chief of a small precinct in Sabt Shimran, as "Sir."

The officer adjusted his manner of sitting in the chair. "Why don't you come back later in the afternoon? There's nothing in your story that calls for immediate action. Go back home; you may find your roommate waiting for you there."

And for a brief moment his words instilled in you the hope that you would find him. But secretly you were annoyed at their disrespectful manner of dismissing you.

You stood up, and, without saying a single word, you rushed out. The heat bounced back off the sidewalks, slammed the houses, fumed on the roads and chased the passers-by.

You said to yourself: "Now, I have to tell her. She has the right to know what's happening."

Her room was no distance, but the fire, which eliminated all shadows, hung immobile, concentrated on the shops closed in waiting for the market day.

You knocked at the door. It was open. In a few moments she was standing in front of you.

She expressed surprise, and said, "Muhammad, what-

22

ever brings you here at this hour?"

Your voice rattled as you replied: "Ustadh Muhammad has disappeared, Fatima."

"What are you saying, Muhammad?"

"I said Ustadh Muhammad has disappeared."

A drowsy voice could be heard inside, saying, "Who are you talking to Fatima?"

"It's Muh . . ."

Before she had time to complete her sentence, you'd disappeared. You vanished completely, leaving Fatima transfixed by a circle of pain.

Behind you, you could hear somebody weeping and weeping.

3

Sabt Shimran resembles stones strewn between two hills of black rock. On entering it you face its east side, perched on the heights of a hill fortified with old castles, studded with stones that shine like knives, deflecting birds into collision courses, magnifying the blueness of the sky and the sun's apogee remorselessly beating down on exposed houses. Sabt Shimran spells out sadness and blood . . . a year of death.

Sometimes, the devastating aura of the place disperses you in the slow hemorrhage of time. You become involved in the irreversible climate of despondency, that emaciated creature devoured by all illnesses from the common cold to cancer, from tuberculosis to influenza.

Sabt Shimran . . . Ustadh Muhammad tried to find in it an extension of his soul. This above all had been his intention.

He'd tried to find a horizon for the place in his heart, only to discover that a mutual aversion was their one link in common.

Windows open out on to heat; the streets are silent.

If a stranger encountered this place, he'd think a war had reduced it to a rubble of stones. An unannounced war between the infiltration of life and the serenity of the dead.

A village like no other village, and we're distributed to small rooms with roofs made out of corn stalks, and doors without locks. We lie in the black of the night in restless sleep, and hear our ribs shatter on waking, before we're re-exposed to fever and a murderous isolation.

Sabt Shimran is the mother village whose emaciated children comb the rugged valleys in the noonday sun, looking for food for their cattle. And on the outskirts of this village are still more dilapidated ruins.

Sabt Shimran ... stony days in stony prairies that stretch for huge distances.

The sun had reached its zenith. It looked like an eagle that scrutinized the earth with its sharp eyes. You were the one estranged creature visible in the streets.

You were scorched by gazing at the center of the sky. Stars revolved with you. You raised your hands to shield yourself from the flames and were surprised by the still greater heat of your forehead.

You said: "It can't be fever," then added as an afterthought, "and why shouldn't it be fever?"

"It's enough my roommate got it, without me falling a prey to it, too."

It hurt you now to think the relationship had never gone beyond that of two people sharing a room. It had

25

always seemed on the brink of something deeper.

You didn't dare look into your heart.

Instead, you looked up at the sun again. That action was like the union of two live embers in the heart of the noon.

In your mind you cursed that policeman for telling his chief we bore the same name. But in the end it would be all right, you assured yourself.

Without warning, a convulsion shook you, threatened to break you, and you had to restrain your whole being, to make sure you didn't say it aloud, that no one had heard it, that it hadn't pierced your skin and spread to the streets and people. Suddenly you asked:

But how did he leave the house? I had to open the door from the inside this morning!

"Yes, I ran, I crossed the small desert between the bed and the door, and turned the key. Yes, with these two hands I turned the key, then went out."

You tried to find, in the walls, another exit large enough for his body. But there was none.

You turned round, thinking of going back to the police precinct. But you froze in your place. The precinct lay silently in the fiery forest.

And that discovery was against you, not against anybody else on the surface of this globe.

So you turned round again.

Between the precinct and the market square, Hanash's shack stood. You knew it well. Then there was Haj al-Ani's shop. He owned shops that joined the prairies and mountains of Tihama with the Red Sea coast.

Wooden boxes, empty juice cans, the traces of temporary shacks, all that had remained of al-Sabt's market. The sun revolved once more, drew near until it touched

26

your body. You walked, and it was aimed at the place between your shoulders like a rifle. You couldn't move any faster. You couldn't stop. You said, as your limbs began to shake:

"Ali, where's Thuraiban?"

He pointed to the north and said, "There."

You said, "Do you have any water?"

"No," he said.

"Give me a bottle of Pepsi."

You drank it and left. You could clearly see in your mind the water bottles lying at the bottom of the gas icebox when he brought out the Pepsi can.

You turned your head. The young boy was staring at you with mischievous eyes. You said:

"But I came from the east, Ali, from this direction."

"Ustadh! I'm a native of this region. I know it well."

You said, "It's possible sometimes for the student to be right and his teacher wrong."

Nothing changes in this village, at least that's what they say. Its expansive hopes are crystallized in a road leading from the city of Jeddah which transects it, connecting it to the pulse-beat of life and a chain of neon gas-stations.

You said, "Tell me, Abu Ali, from where we're standing, in what direction does Thuraiban lie?"

He pointed to the south.

"There, at the bottom of the mountain, Ustadh."

You said, "But Ali pointed to the north!"

"What ignorance, Ustadh. Ali is very young, but we are natives of these parts, and couldn't mislead you."

You said, "Then I'll walk."

"Sit down, Ustadh," he said, "you won't be able to reach it now."

"I'll try," you said.

Thuraiban's the village in which my roommate and I live. We're the only teachers in the community. Perhaps it was to protect the honor of its voluptuous women that Sabt Shimran put us on a hill two miles away.

You questioned an old man coming out of the mosque as to the whereabouts of Thuraiban.

He said, "Over there, son," and pointed to the west. No matter how you juggled north, south and west in your mind, they wouldn't form a composite picture. You waited for two hours not daring to ask further directions to Thuraiban. You feared the next person you questioned would say it lay to the east, near those palm trees. And the trees were of course an illusion.

4

You scanned the horizon searching for a dust-cloud that would mean a car crossing the wilderness, but there was nothing. Fatigue registered in your feet; sharp stones and the burning sand scoured them.

You sat down.

You were isolated like the one visible palm. Its shade was powerless to impart coolness to the sand.

It was Amara day. Cars returning from there have to cross the area around Sabt Shimran in the direction of Thuraiban. It was at this hour that traffic would begin leaving the hubbub of the Tuesday market, with its confused bartering.

In this vast wilderness, villages lie scattered without any harmony, drawn together by the polarization of similar magnets. Their one common meeting point is the attraction of market-days.

Saturday is for Sabt Shimran, Sunday for Namira, Monday for Sirr Bani al-Muntashir, Tuesday for Amara, Wednesday for Inkhal, Thursday for Mikhwah and Friday for God . . . and . . .

The market is a common meeting-place, people congregate around the small shacks which depart at noon for the following day's market, and meet again over the rising prices of dates or the lowered price of camels, or the wooden jugs of butter and inhale the women's perfume. And everywhere there are colors: black for old women, yellow and orange for young women and white for men.

From a long way off a cloud of dust was approaching like a giant taken up by a mad kind of dance, rising in a spiral until its head disappeared in the sky. It drove towards you and you signaled. It stopped and the cloud of dust eventually dispersed so that you could see the jeep clearly.

The voice of "al-Qahim," that singer so admired by all truck drivers and jeep owners, hit you with his song, although you were unable to decipher its words. You imagined the dust giant couldn't have elevated himself to such improbable heights without the accompaniment of that inspiration—and that the dance was a reality and not a figment of your deranged imagination.

Al-Qahim continued to sing, the notes voluble, the pauses occurring between lines, the voice taken down into the depths before being released as a high note.

Despite your efforts you couldn't make sense of the song, for the fluctuations of the voice eluded your ear.

He sang to no accompaniment, a voice that was as rugged as this landscape of stones, crows, hawks and hungry wolves which had contributed to his origin.

The driver lowered the volume control and you were able to ask:

"Are you going towards Thuraiban?"

"We're heading for the Sawad, Ustadh."

You thanked him and he turned up the volume. Al-Qahim's voice which you felt was unsuccessfully trying to come out of the tape, rose for a last time within the field of your hearing. The dust giant resumed his dance.

In the distance you could make out the figure of a policeman, one of the two from the precinct. He seemed to come forward carried by the wind. He hung suspended, contracting distances, and approached you.

"I'm arresting you," he said, pointing at you with his finger, and raising his hand as if aiming a pistol at the spot between your eyes.

"Why?"

"You're accused of killing your companion, Hammad."

"Have you found his body?"

"No."

"Have you been to Thuraiban? I doubt it."

"No."

"Have you investigated the matter?"

"No. All the evidence points to you."

"How can you accuse me in such a detached manner?"

"I'm not accusing you. You killed him. The chief says you must have hidden your roommate's corpse."

"But that's a grave accusation, one which would lead to my death."

"Couldn't care less."

The policeman drew nearer, and entered the circle of shade.

"Do you intend to take me to the precinct?"

"Yes," he said.

"You've got to catch me first," you said, as you started to run away.

No sooner had you started to run than you realized the restrictions imposed by a *dashdash*. You looked around you, hitched up the rim of the gown and began running like a horse. This created in you the impression of running at an even greater speed than you really were.

"He'll only find me when I'm dead," you told yourself.

But everything now had changed. You'd hardly reached the western end of Sabt Shimran when you discovered you weren't the only person running. There were women in flight, children screaming, and men grinding the stones with their bare feet.

It was as if the southern hill had exploded, throwing everything to the sky—houses, people, the sun and the crows. A spontaneous combustion. You wondered:

"Do the police want to arrest us all?"

When the crowd stopped running your instinct was to hide among them.

The old man said, "Make way, make way."

And you saw a well. You hadn't forgotten it.

"Who's willing to go down?" a voice said.

"But tell us what's happening. What's going on."

"Abdallah fell into that well. He was filling the water tank with gas and the tank plummeted down. He climbed down to get it, and he's still there."

Motors were installed in the middle of wells, and the connecting pipes fed into cement reservoirs. Hanash the baker volunteered to go down.

He took off his slippers and wedged the edge of his

gown in his teeth. He held on to the large stone at the top of the well and slipped down effortlessly like a snake.

The policeman forgot all about you.

Everyone held their breath.

"What can you see, Hanash?"

"Nothing. I can't see anything."

"Get away from the edge of the well, all of you," the old man shouted, "you're in the light." As he shouted his eyes dilated and veins protruded from his forehead.

"What do you see, Hanash?"

"Nothing. Are you sure Abdallah's in here?" Abdallah's wife shrieked, and his mother struck her cheeks. There was a noise of someone entering the water, then you could hear Hanash swimming.

"Have you found anything?"

The sounds grew confused, then the well appeared to narrow and the crowd grow silent.

The water reverted to its calm, and fear was apparent in the men's faces. The women stifled their screams, and the children backed off.

"Why don't you answer, Hanash?"

The echo reverberated, came back in circles, and then it seemed that the voice too had dropped into the water. With his thick mustache, and a beard that covered the lower part of his chin, the tall figure of the chief of police made its way through the crowd. He was still yawning and showing evidence of his clothes being stuck to his body, which told me he hadn't left his seat since I saw him. He approached the well. As soon as the old man saw him, he took him by the hand and pointed to the darkness at the bottom of the well. The chief of police looked confused. A profusion of cold sweat covered his body.

The old man said, "What are you going to do now, Jabir? Both Abdallah and Hanash are down there."

The chief of police fixed his eyes into the dark. His lethargy was evaporating, being replaced by visible embarrassment. Before he had time to answer, the voice of fat Abd al-Rahman said assertively, "Tie me to a rope. I'll go down."

The features of the chief of police relaxed, then reassumed their customary contorted expression. He had the look of someone who was powerless to restrain his anxiety.

You remembered how Ustadh Muhammad used to say to you: "Ustadh Muhammad, ever since I got to know this land and the *mutawwi* came out at me with his stick, driving me towards the mosque, I've never found any difference between a religious *shaikh* and a policeman."

Abd al-Rahman's body was heavy, but his spirit was light. He was a good-hearted man who knew how to smile, and how to brave danger. He was courageous.

He dangled at the end of the rope. Under other circumstances, had he been able to view his own body hanging from a rope, he would have laughed until his veins burst.

Little by little . . .

The rope was lowered slowly, and Abd al-Rahman tried to find a grip on the circumference of the well. But the stone was smooth and slippery as soap. And the grasses that grew from the wall-crevices were far too fragile to cope with the weight of a body intent on plumbing the unknown.

A few moments later, we heard Abd al-Rahman shouting from the interior.

"I can't see anything."

The *shaikh* called for a lantern, but before it could be brought to the big man's assistance he plunged through the water into the heart of darkness.

They lowered the lantern into the well.

The chief of police's eyes bulged. His mouth gaped open.

The *shaikh* shouted, "Lower the lantern carefully."

Little by little . . .

There was a pause before the explosion.

The women retreated and the men were shaken. Children looked on with surprise and the policeman backed away from his chief. When Abd al-Rahman rose to the surface again, it was on a wave of terror, and two stiff bodies could be seen floating on the water's film.

It must be the gas . . .

Suddenly Abd al-Rahman lost his balance and went under.

The old man shouted, "Pull the rope."

Hands clasped the rope, which began to respond to the concerted effort.

The three lifeless bodies that lay around the well presented an enigma. After separating in the depths they'd come together on the surface, looking for impossible answers. What had brought this about was a gallon of gas, burns, a hallucinatory storm, a series of departures, panting breath.

"Abdallah's still breathing," someone shouted.

The shout was accompanied by the joyful hysteria of Abdallah's wife, while the screams of Abd al-Rahman's wife and children intensified in pitch. Hanash retreated to his shack, forgotten, his arm lifted in the air, a broken signal to which no-one responded, but his sister, Aliyya, the one human being who cared.

Many were weeping, and the rest of the villagers ran out to the well. They packed around its rim and intermingled with the shocked crowd. People pressed around Abd al-Rahman's wife.

There was an abrupt silence. Only an explosion like this could have submerged those voices.

Spray flashed out of the well as a body broke the surface of the water.

"Who's fallen down?" you asked.

You felt you alone were conscious of what had just taken place. No one replied.

"It's Muhammad Hammad," you shouted, conscious you could never return with a gallon of gas.

Another crash.

"Who's fallen down?"

You said, "It's him, it's him. . . ."

Fulmination after fulmination followed. Detonations of spray.

Then your own body started its slow descent into the mound of corpses that blocked the well, before making contact with the water and the smell of gas that hung in the dark.

There were half-hearted rescue attempts. You penetrated the layer of corpses . . . gas . . . water . . . terror . . . death. The air burned. The odor of gas grew stronger. When the rope was pulled away you breathed again. It was the breath of life.

That emaciated body hung suspended and, before blacking out completely, you were soaring at the crest of the shaft.

You didn't know how long you had remained on the rope, caught there like an awkward doll, only that it seemed that all the surrounding villages, the desert, the houses, the people, and the birds from the savage north, were straining to pull you in.

You woke up.

You said, out loud: "I can still run, I've got some breath left, and two feet and a day's start."

The chief of police approached the policeman who'd pursued you.

"Did you catch him?" he asked.

"No."

"And why not, you fool?"

"You've seen what's happened."

"And where is he?"

But before he had time to point at you you were running again like a wooden horse, your chest pushed forward to allow your head to swing freely, and your feet to dance over the sand. And while you ran Ustadh Muhammad's mental image burnt itself into the unfathomable regions of your unconscious.

He had on occasions talked to you about things that had happened to him in the course of his long life, beginning with his graduation, his unemployment, and touching on his work in building construction and his stories about cement and hot iron rods.

And listening to these stories, you were most often struck by their similarities to your own life experience, so much so that it could have been you who'd lived them.

You'd even gone so far as to say to him one day, "You're exaggerating, Ustadh Muhammad. Didn't I tell you the story you're now repeating to me?" But he swore to its authenticity, even though you knew it was yours.

And now, in the incandescent noon he was running at your side.

You asked him: "Which one of us is being chased by the police?"

He said, "It's me they want."

And you replied, "No, it's me. If I were to stop, they'd catch me and let you go free."

"You're wrong," he said. "It's me they're after."

(A Scene)

He eyed the street with caution before letting himself out of the door. As soon as he was quite sure there was no danger, he'd go on to his work.

This habit, of proceeding with extreme wariness, had become part of his behavior ever since the day fear had made the sweat stand out on his forehead, and the sun had gathered into a ball between his shoulders.

The sun disappeared behind a high cloud. He gathered the sides of his black coat and went on to hum a folk song, but stopped, as soon as the thought struck him that the best way to escape was by running away.

He heard familiar voices behind him. His heart accelerated rapidly, the pulse throbbing in his arteries, as it dawned on him who these people were. His pace quickened, involuntarily, until he was running head over heels, like a wooden horse.

He used to claim that he loved to run this way!

He heard the sound of claws flickering across the

surface of the road, and repeated to himself, "The best way to escape is by running away."

All his accumulated fear drove him on. When he looked round to assure himself of the distance he'd placed between himself and the pack, one of the dogs hurled itself at him, ripping the coat off his body.

The morning was cool, but he couldn't feel it. Another dog jumped behind him and tore off his shirt.

They'd spare me nothing.

A deadness settled in his lungs.

A third dog leapt to bring down his emaciated bleeding body.

Another dog, and another, and another . . .

In the course of his daylong flight he realized that he was completely naked, but he couldn't stop running. When he finally summoned the courage to look back, the dogs had disappeared.

He went back home in the evening. Rain spat at his body, seeped on to his face, blurred his eyes, and rolled down to his toes.

The silence was oppressive. It was broken by a soft laughter that froze in his ears.

"Where are your clothes?"

"The dogs have torn them off."

"You were running away from them, then?"

"How did you know?"

"Because it's obvious you've been pursued, and that teeth have lacerated your body."

The little one continued to laugh for eight months. The sound of that voice tormented you, that swollen place in your memory that wouldn't let you breathe normally.

(Curtain)

Again he began to run. A dark night and big distances opening up towards the south.

"I think you were with me that night," he said.

"Yes," you replied.

We ran away together. The night, the sound of scores of dogs, then, suddenly, the day broke revealing a desert and a scorching sun. From the north came the sound of sad reverberating laughter.

You said, "Ustadh Muhammad, it was I who ran and you who kept pace beside me."

He said, "No, it was I who ran and you who trailed by my side."

You were able to elude the policeman. Then at last you stopped. Your eyes drank in the horizon on all sides. Blood was pouring from your feet, your body was torn by spears, and the evening was engulfing you.

You said, "If they want to arrest me, let them do it here, at home. And if they want to cut my head off, let it at least remain as clear as possible."

> With a cloud's buoyant calm I tempt the river
> And the birds
> And the sea.
> I evoke the lost years
> Traces of childhood written on my features
> And repeat my prayer
> Alone
> And climb
> Whispering between knocking on the door
> And the sorrow hammering in my pulse.

-Am I late? . . . No.
I climb
Looking for a rose that's not there,
Gathering the winds to my stride.
One step
After another
And in the silence I raise my foot
And knock on the door
No sound
I knock
Enter
And find everything still the same.
I smile
Lay my blood on the bed
And stare at the ceiling
Footsteps are still pacing the sands
Forever approaching.
I whisper, again,
-Am I late?
But he does not answer
He moves here, in the air
And here
But does not answer.
And the footsteps advance,
Draw nearer
And nearer
The desert expands
The iron trembles in my hands
My life shakes in his palms
And when I try to shout
My voice is inaudible.

A few brief illuminated thoughts, then the fire thunders in your skull, and you lie unconscious.

5

The night . . . streets, faces . . . goats and shepherds, snakes crawling in search of the shade, and lights that aren't yet on. Stories await the telling; there are figures whose shadows have receded, and stars you can count by focusing on the sky from your position in the room.

You would have felt your head to be sure it was still there, only you couldn't make contact with your hands to lift them to your head.

The heat fires your blood, names get mixed up, streets misidentified. Everything blurs. Your body periscopes like a worn headstone, which would gladly take refuge beneath the earth. You lose all sense of coordination. You're thrown into a state of unrelieved chaos, which raises its walls around you. But first of all you must find your hands, before you attempt to emerge from a hole you don't see. You need to have a finger or an arm, a shoulder or a leg, before you can take the offensive.

Walls reach up into the impenetrable black, then slowly subside, before disappearing, leaving only the ceiling and the lance-heads of the darkness above you.

Was it necessary, you kept on asking yourself, for your roommate to disappear and leave you to your death? Did he have to go?

You wanted the earth to open and swallow you. Yes, the earth is the only thing able to accommodate this destruction, this progressive fire, this absent presence, this existence that borders on nothingness. Only the earth can assimilate this.

It occurred to you that perhaps the earth had devoured him. The idea terrified you. You came face to face with the solid darkness, dreading to encounter what you couldn't bear.

It took courage to reopen your eyes and fix your stare on the ceiling. You succeeded. You were still capable of moving. It mattered little if the movement emanated from the hand, the foot, the tremor of an eye. The important thing to realize was, you're still alive . . . you're still alive!

You stared at the ground, at the gulf which had opened between two iron beds. It terrified you to see that rift expand.

You would have liked to take the decisive step and leave your body behind, and be done with all it entailed. By an inverse motion you would have liked to dive to the depths of the earth in the way astronauts climb into outer space. You couldn't be sure any longer as to his where-abouts. He might have been projected beyond the frontiers of the earth. But you were sad, sad.

"May you be blown across the face of the desert," I found myself thinking. "No matter, I'll always love you, for you're a part of me, my inner self. I'm the one who's an outsider. You could break into my interior but you wouldn't find yourself there. You'd meet with a hollow like the space inside a porcelain jar. Come back to me and we'll depart together. You need me. I know you'll cross frontiers carrying no identity card, owning to no name, and outlawed wherever you go. But you'll suffer all the same, for the significant reason that an insignificant little policeman, one evening, neglected to ask your name, or pay any attention to you ... Your sorrow will come by realizing you're incomplete without me."

You put your head back on the pillow. The sea ran in your direction. Wave after wave broke over you. You were enveloped by a sea infested with white sharks—voracious killers that would beach your mutilated body. Can you swim?

You would have run, but there was no place of refuge. The sea recedes only to reveal a desert patrolled by wolves and foxes. Snakes crouch under the long night. Attack comes from every horizon.

Nothing can help our vulnerability in the face of death. I felt I had to break through the monotonous sand-dunes if I was to see the sky, not that I have any feeling of affinity with the latter. Perhaps it was the earth I wanted to see. Its surface can be green, alive with gazelles, birds and wild rabbits. Wolves, panthers, tigers, hyenas fulfill their function on earth, and even the tubercular go on living. There are murderers, and there's Thuraiban, but that doesn't matter. I want to see the earth, because it's beautiful.

45

The desert's widened. It's always crawling in our direction. We scream, and then crawl towards it and find a point of intersection. We clash, look around us and discover we're still alive.

The desert passes through us. It's as if we'd broken it, penetrated it with the point of a spear. The sea continues to run, the desert widens, and which of them rolls over us?

You learn to watch their approach with a child's eyes, this dual thunder-head which threatens to annihilate you. Your body disintegrates. Your scream disperses into shrapnel.

A last attempt . . . You try to piece your body together. You g . . . et up, then fall again.

You lean on the table and sway under your own weight. How many times had you told your roommate not to consign you to solitude. You'd spoken to him of your fear of white ants and how they collected on the table. They eat and kill without our ever seeing it. They leave a residue of paper-thin skeletons that crumble to ash.

When you told him ants were crawling inside the table-legs, his response was to advise you to sit with your feet raised from the floor. "At any rate, they won't eat you," he said.

"But why not?" I asked. "Is the table more appetizing than my flesh?"

You should have looked for a stable support in a shadow or a wall, a cane or a memory. You should have got up. As a last attempt, you placed your hand in the middle of the table. You wanted to be sure of the presence of some greenery, and that the window overlooked trees, familiar faces. You would have liked to see familiar faces before returning to your oven-bed.

Your feet are on the floor; the palm of your hand on the middle of the table. For a moment the table becomes a sand-dune, a viscid mound that you plunge your hand into. And why should you express regret at its disappearance, at its being unwilling any longer to support your sardine-can, your can of chickpea-spread, the loaf of bread. Better to let it all go, its rotten fabric not even worthy of upholding those few utensils. Your hand spontaneously drew back. Your fingers had during this time been plunged into a mound of white ants which had begun to climb your arm. You shook that arm with a force that might have separated it from your body. The ants must be made to retreat, they eat whole villages, tables, roofs, but they can't eat people.

Without warning he materialized in front of you. He pointed to the ant-train climbing your arm, and his laughter reverberated: "Ants have eaten you at last, they've worked into your wooden frame."

You advance. His figure increases in height. You try to get a grip on his neck, but his figure spirals up with such rapidity that you find yourself clutching his leg.

He continues to laugh. You push his leg. You take two steps back in order to see him, but he disappears. You look around and find you're alone, and instinctively move towards the door. Voices echo from the distant ravines where black rocks rise against the black night. They approach. You're reduced to slow-motion: ants are everywhere. You'll never live this time again, but you're saturated with its details, with its oppressive shadows.

The door shakes, the world rocks at a new intrusion . . . the stone-walls, the sacks of white corn rock. When you mentioned to Amm Saud that the room was now a living-place and not a store-house, he said, "Ustadh Muhammad, the room's large. It's big enough for a playground." But you can't remember who it was who spoke to him; it might have been the other Muhammad. I don't know.

The room's wide. If it wasn't for fear of damnation, I'd have sworn it's as wide as half an airport. The airport accommodates Westerners, men who are searching for metals in the Aseer mountains, and these mountains so rich in natural resources are uninhabited by us. We're hollow and yet the mountains live in us, and they who embody everything are empty of us.

The airport comprises a piece of land, alternately wide and narrow, sands that have petrified, and white stones at the sides.

"Don't worry, Amm Saud. The sacks will remain here, not only in the room, but in our hearts as well."

You took one step, and another. You shook your arm for the last time. You looked for the flashlight, and the matches, but both had disappeared. The knocks increased with renewed violence.

You said, "Who is it?"

They said, "It's us."

You replied, "I'm coming then."

You surmised it was the police. If they wanted your head, they could have waited until the morning. You needed to sleep. You were tired, and very sad.

Once again you considered putting on your *dashdash*, but you recalled how it had failed to induce respect on

48

their first visit. This time it might be necessary to run away.

Five faces without any features surrounded you.

"Yes, what is it you want?"

"Have you changed your mind about the thousand *riyals*?"

"What thousand *riyals*?"

"Those we asked you to pay towards the cost of your burial." I laughed out loud—it was a way of convincing myself I was still alive and functioning.

I stopped in order to intensify the silence, then began laughing again, on and on without pause. Laughter fit to last a lifetime.

"You seem happy tonight. Why keep on pretending that you aren't dead?"

"You've simply mistaken the man you want to see."

"How?"

"Because I'm not the roommate for whom you're searching." The silence closed in again. They stepped forward, whispering, then let out a collective laugh, one so perfect you would have thought it rehearsed.

"You can't delude us. You're looking for a way to convince us you're someone else, in order to avoid payment. You're stingy. We told you yesterday you've got to pay tonight."

The circle tightened. "But I'm not him," I protested.

"Where is he then," they questioned, "hiding inside?"

"No!" I said.

"You dumb corpse," they retorted, and kicked me heavily in the thigh.

"But I swear I'm not him," I said.

"Then what's your name?" they asked.

49

"Muhammad Hammad," I said.

"And what's his name?" they questioned.

I realized that I was falling into the same trap again, and must avoid it at all costs.

"This is a conspiracy," I said.

When they questioned me again, their words crackled angrily. "What's your name?"

"Muhammad," I replied.

"Muhammad what?"

"Muhammad Hammad," I answered.

"We were right after all. You've no choice but to pay."

"But I'm not the person you want," I pleaded.

"That doesn't matter," they replied. "It doesn't matter at all. Seeing that you're dead, names are irrelevant. If there's a case of mistaken identity, it's all the same to us. To justify yourself you have only to pay your burial costs like all the others have done. They've contributed while still alive. A man is remembered by his funeral."

"Am I dead?" I asked, growing increasingly confused by their manner of speech.

"Yes," they answered. "You're no longer alive."

"And you want a thousand *riyals* from me?"

"Yes, we need a thousand *riyals*."

"And will you go away after that?"

"Yes."

"And I won't see you again?"

"How could you, you fool, when you're dead?"

The embers had almost died down completely, although a number continued to twinkle. One step, two, the bed, the briefcase . . . you tripped on something, probably the pot, judging by the discharge of liquid, and you felt something sticky on your legs.

50

You cursed your double for not emptying the pot. For four days the *mulukhiyya* had been left to grow stagnant.

Due to the increase of light, it was easier for you to find your way back to the door.

"This is for you," I said.

"A thousand *riyals?*" they answered in unison.

"Yes, that's the sum you requested. It's all I have. Go and do whatever you want."

They lined up courteously, and with extreme politeness approached me, and shook hands with me one after the other. Then they embraced me as a group.

"Thanks," they said. "You can be assured the funeral will be worthy of you."

I felt the insult all the more acutely, as I sensed they meant the opposite.

"Goodbye."

"Goodbye."

Their engines roared and simultaneously their lights came on. Foxes scurried for shelter, their luminous eyes drilling holes in the dark. My white hen fidgeted, and the cock scrutinized the light, but remained silent.

"Thank God, I'm rid of them, and of Ustadh Muhammad's legacy," I thought to myself. "They'll never return here now, but they'll track him down and bury him."

I crept into the privacy of my bed.

6

How many nights must pass before this one expires? Will you ever again experience the benevolent dream of a sunrise? Will you ever discover where your companion disappeared to?

You can't understand why you feel tenderness for him now, why his image flutters in your eyes like a dreamy bird. You can be sure now that he's disappeared, for had they found his body, they wouldn't have returned tonight. Your senses are so heightened, you can almost trace the dust his footsteps raised in this room, and hear him turn the key silently before going out on tiptoe. But how, how?

You ask yourself why he had to dislocate the iron door, and let out a scream in the face of the unendurable, the treeless shade? Did he have to climb the summit of the black mountain and announce his rebellion?

His disappearance opens up blue spaces. His going is as benevolent as his original coming.

You can recall his face with clarity: his eyes, his sadness at the time of your first meeting on this burning carpet on which both of you had tried to escape. In the end only one of you did.

When you contemplated him you added your own age to his features. Another thirty years and both of you would be as old as the fatigue that lives in your cells. The distance separating you was encapsulated in a single word: the desert.

After a while you shook off the dust that covered your face . . . and your words. And no sooner had you both regained your features than the future seemed bright again.

But the sense of absence persisted. The nagging suspicion returned that perhaps he had indeed dislocated the door from its hinges, climbed the black summit of the mountain, encamped there, and left you to conjecture as to his whereabouts. He alone knows the secret of his disappearance, the ratio between absence and presence.

You wondered what had caused his sudden wish to leave. More than once you'd assured him, "We don't need much to survive here."

In reply he used to say: "We need a free spirit, our presence must be felt in the places we inhabit, and I don't feel that here. We don't exist when the place refuses to acknowledge our presence."

You'd carried baggage on your journey south, and now the whole region seemed to contribute to your vagrancy, your estrangement.

This is al-Qunfudhah then
a city full of water
a place without a sea
a city without land
the desolation of sand
buries everything.

Lost in that place you look for your pockets—you search for your self and find it extinguished. The feeling is that a bullet has clean-holed your memory.

You might have amused yourself by remembering the time you sat in the rear of a jeep, cradled on ice that was being shipped from Jeddah to al-Qunfudhah to be sold by the pound. The driver seemed to overtake the stars, then fall back behind them, and all the while the singer's voice seemed to reach us from outer space. He had to reach al-Qunfudhah before the sun rose and melted the ice.

Or you might amuse yourself by crying. What difference does it make? When the *mutawwi* enters and opening the door of the mosque just after midnight, screams,

You can sleep there, at the seashore,
But is there a shore to this sea?

Ibn Abdo will beat his head on the ground and pray, then raise his eyes and scrutinize you, before continuing with his prayer. And when you attempt to leave, he cuts short his prayer and addresses you in soft, oily tones. His spies in the Education Department told him you have five thousand *riyals*.

An iron bed, a mattress, a pot, some plates, a stove, these are all your possessions. And twenty cans of sardines, ten of beans, five of cooked broad beans and five of chickpeas, the entire amount worth perhaps two thousand *riyals*. Enough for a voyage to the Amazon or to the Himalayas?

You sign at the bottom of the page, entrusting Ibn Abdo with your deposit and rent, trusting that he'll return the former to you. You know in the end it will be a hard struggle, that even after your fifth letter he won't send the balance to you and won't forget to charge you an extra five percent for his labor.

You'd dreamt of holding the five thousand *riyals* in your own hands, but that wasn't to be. The jealousy of others would have found a way of denying you this pleasure.

Ibn Abdo returns to the prayer he'd cut short, and to watching the shop door again, and the arrival of dust covered faces.

The Aseer mountains wade into the distance. Despite the absence of a sea they have water, humidity, freshness, fertility of land.

The earth bites at your feet; it's come to inhabit you. The horizon circles with its sparse palms, thorns and cactus, crows, scorpions and monkeys. It will be a long undeclared war between you and the earth to decide which one of you will bury the other so as to go on living. But you don't have the strength to assume this conflict alone.

Although the relationship had lacked the time to deepen, the long, dark nights you'd shared in each other's company were a sort of assurance of familiarity.

For some unexplained reason I noticed how terror distorted his features whenever I drew close. Did he really fear me that much? I don't remember ever having offended him. Perhaps it was a wrongly placed word, a small, seemingly insignificant thing that led to his suspicion. If I think back I can remember the origin of his mistrust.

I said, "I'm starting to get accustomed to life here together." Then I corrected myself. "No," I said, "I'm on my way to getting accustomed to the things that surround us here."

After that, our discourse tended towards silence and the agony of the long road we traveled together towards the school. We virtually had to collide with each other in order to prompt a "good morning" or "good evening," although the expressions gave you an indication of the hostility that existed between us.

The affection between the two of you never ceased, you can't deny that. You needed a special sorrow to unite you, and a special joy.

But his character possessed a good characteristic of yours, although you were powerless to tame the bird that soared within you both. You held your peace; any declaration of affection would have been misconstrued.

You were familiar with loneliness by now, in the same way his spirit had achieved the mastery of a bird in flight. In his absence, only your scream asserts a presence in this desolate place, telling him to move still further away despite his fatigue, the good that goes with him. Your one hope is that no one finds him before you do. You climb to the high summit and shriek into a wind that carries your agonized alarm. The winds are obedient to your dictates, and the valleys serve as an echo-chamber to your voice. Storms gather in the ravine-caves, extracting stones, up-rooting trees, but still there's no sign of him.

You're averse to the winds; their insistent, blustering

hum always leaves you disturbed. They beat their secret wings around you in the high places, and tear at your frail body.

Buffeted by them, you run down the other side of the mountain, the wind at your heels, searching to trip you, ballooning your shirt like a flag whipped from the mast-head.

RUN! you shout as the whole pack closes on you. And in the wildness of your flight, you think, "The winds won't be able to catch him when they're on my tail." A roar of thunder, and torrential rains beat down from the sky-face. It's as though the sea had got into the sky as though the sea were here, but no water, as though the sands were here, but no land. RUN!

The sheep get up to higher grazing, and lower down there are only camels trapped by the torrent, and a few herdsmen trying to save them. In the end the drowned camels will be ditched on muddy shores.

Nothing could break the speed of your flight. You're determined to outstrip the elements, to overtake the flood. Your call-note comes out again in the form of a scream—RUN!—for the winds are after you. And the mountains carry the echo from one to the other.

Water runs profusely down your face—rivulets stream from your neck. But despite the deluge you're happy Ustadh Muhammad's escaped the whirlpool. You'd be happier if he returned, and sad if he stayed. You try to imagine living for even a day without his bird.

The flood smashes at your heels and your shirt flies. This could be death at last. Al-Qunfudhah silently disappears behind the bends of the valley, its black stone resolute against the thunder, its children awaiting their destruction.

7

The wind had collected its spears and taken refuge in its secret chambers at the base of the mountains, under the large volcanic rocks, between the hills. Part of it climbed the Aseer peaks, and the rest veered off in the direction of Bisha. Its aftermath was sudden, unpredictably violent gusts, like stray bullets.

You felt no calm in the storm's abatement. Acute tension had kept you suspended on that thin dividing line between dissociation and death.

Although it was close to dawn the sky remained dark. Lonely points of light showed here and there, and the landscape glowered with burning hallucination.

Another body hit the water, dowsing your face with a bloody drizzle of spray. Another victim, and you shout, "Who's fallen?"

"Is it you, Ustadh Muhammad?"

". . . . ."

Someone plummets into the gasoline-filmed water. Blood flies in the air, big spots of it. Once again the burning stones are crawling away from the sun. You feel hollow; a vessel to be filled by the wind. You search for trees, for people, for stone houses and shacks . . . but there's no sign of any people, just that one shack shaped like a clown's hat, empty, performing without a head. The shack's stuck in the ground like a stake that's been used to impale people, a stake, that settled at last between the shoulders of the one human being you caught sight of before he disappeared.

You don't know for certain he's disappeared, or perhaps you were determined not to see, or even transfer him back to the imagination or admit him into a dream.

For a long time you relied on dream to acquaint you with reality and the ground beneath your feet, and now this tangible foundation seemed empty of everything, including you: it had become a thorny wilderness, an internalized landscape of nightmare.

It's a depressing thing to wave your hands in an empty landscape. And to find yourself saturated, but so far removed from the sea, the drops beading your forehead spelling out flames and ice, duality, stabs of fever, the hallucinatory abyss.

It came to meet you, the sound of a truck's horn on the road to Jizan and south to Najran. Thousands of trucks would follow, carrying tuberculosis, anemia, flour and the yellow ends of old newspapers. A hawk turned round in the sky and plummeted like an arrow on to the earth. It would go on killing hour after hour, hanging motionless before aligning its death-bolt.

The hawks have their own game, we have our own terror, when the human body's alone, like a spirit that's pursued. "Amm Saud, escape with your hands intact, throw the hawk whatever food you're carrying. It won't leave you alone anyway. Hawks are like that. They're indomitable; they tear meat from the bone, pouncing audaciously, gathering their wings, aiming with unfailing precision. If you hadn't sighted the hawk soaring in the sky, it might have appeared a stone had fallen from space, a projectile delivered by Saturn. There was an ecstasy in such accomplishment of killing."

"Staying here isn't easy, Doctor," I found myself saying. The doctor works here eleven months a year, including the harsh summer months, when the teachers leave and nothing inhabits these incandescent villages other than cacti and Ahmad Lutfi.

"Muhammad," the doctor said, "It's not easy to get to Thuraiban. Here there are at least people; there you'll be alone; here you can find shelter from the heat in the shade of houses, there the sun's remorseless. Here we have mail and a Saturday market and education, while in Thuraiban there's nothing. Not even a school." And listening to this, you realized for the first time how much the doctor valued mail and the presence of teachers.

For two full months you had abandoned the idea of being a good human being. You'd always believed you were good, loving, capable of leading people.

The jeep that brings the mail from the remote north, picks up on the saline air of al-Qunfudhah, then pushes on towards Sabt Shimran, Namira, Inkhal, Balharith and Amara.

60

"Today the mail will arrive."

"Has the mail arrived?"

"No . . . the mail will arrive today."

"Are you expecting an important letter?"

"No . . . but I'm expecting the mail. It's possible the letter I sent hasn't arrived yet."

"Then why are you waiting?"

"Yes, why am I waiting? Sometimes I feel it's still here. It just seems like that, although I don't pretend to know. Living is inseparable from imagining.

"But why shouldn't I wait? Everyone else does, and they go on waiting all their lives. You kill time in order to wait for the empty expectation of the mail. Harkan al-Shimrani will approach from the village, sounding his jeep's horn. He'll throw the mail-sack on the ground, and everyone will tear it open."

"This is for you."

"This is for me."

"These aren't for us."

"This has come to the wrong place."

"This has been returned to the doctor."

No, doctor, it's not easy to stay here all these years. Don't get too familiar with this place; all your letters will end up being returned. And knowing this, Harkan al-Shimrani would smile as he drank tea outside, in the cool shade of the doctor's room.

"I've brought you something you'll like."

You look into each other's eyes and wait for him to reveal what he's hiding.

"I won't tell you!"

"Is it something in a bag?"

"Yes."

61

"Is it food?"

"No."

"Is it made of paper and ink and news and pictures . . . and nausea?"

"Yes."

"It's the newspapers then."

You didn't know who was speaking. The morning had the same capacity as the night to hide features. At great speed you rush to the trunk of the car and unload it.

"Calmly, Ustadh, calmly . . ."

In a few moments the newspapers are piled on the ground, showing their cold headlines, their news paragraphs, their pictures. Ustadh Muhammad stared at a paper before saying: "There's an invasion of South Lebanon."

"South Lebanon!?"

"And what does it say of the war's progress?"

"That it's over."

"How can the fighting be over when you say there's an invasion of South Lebanon?"

"Because this paper's three weeks old."

"Never mind that, tell me what it says."

But it's the same old story. Roses arrive in a scorched state, letters lose their warmth from being carried across the desert night, corpses arrive in a state of putrefaction, and news of a war reaches us after a truce has been called.

"Ustadh Muhammad, here's another paper. It's only a week old."

"It doesn't matter anyway."

"Why not?"

"I don't like reading the papers. I never like reading them."

Ustadh Muhammad changed that day. And you changed too.

You remember now how you loved to read the papers the day they were published. This has become a wish now.

As the tedious momentum of a day begins, you catch yourself committing the unforgivable crime of counting the minutes! New interminable days will come again, when September air's shot with red embers and the sun burning until midnight. And then the tension will re-assert itself inside, and there'll be no one to tell you, "There's an opening in these walls."

The doctor said, "We've no solution but to go to Aunt Saliha." You thought over his suggestion. The only person who could have undertaken that journey with you was Ustadh Muhammad; but now you're unable to leave this flaming place together, and the only thing that could affect this union was a place.

> This is al-Qunfudhah
> a city full of water
> a place without a sea
> a city without a land
> the desolation of sand
> buries everything.

There was no hope of finding land there. The torrential floods had pursued a path of annihilation, everything had been swept away. This is al-Qunfudhah .. a place that's capable of splitting a man in half, so how can there be a hope of unity in this divided place.

The doctor repeated, "We've no solution but to go to

Aunt Saliha." You didn't even ask who Aunt Saliha was, but followed the doctor on the dirt road that went across the plains to Jizan, where the eagles come out of the sky like jumbo-jets, swoop on their prey and return to the sky like jets.

She was stretched out on the long wooden chair, made of straw, taking refuge in the shade. The heat intermittently found her body, and then she'd push her chair into the shade.

Aunt Saliha . . . somebody's aunt . . . seventy years old, lying on a wooden bed, wearing clothes in which many colors danced, her features hardened by the ravages of time. Time leaves the most inerasable footprints; it chooses a face for its map.

In the large shack, truck-drivers sprawled on the floor, drinking tea and smoking nargilas. This place is a tea-room, a stop-off dive, and a hotel that faces out to violent sand-storms.

Salima's rippling black skin moves amongst them; small nose, a small mouth, a tall figure dressed in yellow. Conscious of her beauty, she flirts with the truck-drivers.

Salima pounces like a hawk after sizing up her prey. Life's hard here, Ustadh, and everyone tries to hold on to something, jealously guarding its orbit.

Aunt Saliha sat up in her chair. She looked like the vitally alive figure cut out of a dream that has the sleeper stumble over himself.

She continued to draw on her nargila.

"Aunt Saliha," the doctor said, "Ustadh's new here, and he needs a room for two or three months."

I was hoping the doctor would say the room was required for both myself and Ustadh Muhammad, but, as I waited for her answer, this reasoning seemed insignificant.

"Doctor," she said, "I no longer rent rooms."

"But it's only for a couple of months at the most," the doctor reasoned, "and he's here for everyone's benefit, after all."

"Go and look for a room at Abu Ali's."

"But Aunt Saliha, you know he doesn't have vacancies."

"How's that, doctor?" she asked. "None of the teachers have arrived so far."

"Ahmad Lutfi's rented every available room in the village."

"And why's that? Does he have twenty families of his own?"

"No," said the doctor, "but he wants to make a profit out of sub-letting."

"Then go and rent a room from him," she replied.

"Aunt Saliha! He rents out his rooms for a year at a time, and the Ustadh's only staying two months on his way to Thuraiban."

"Doctor, you're dear to me, but I . . ."

"A month or two at the most . . ."

The hawk revolved, then dropped, taking its prey up towards the sun.

The land was like a skeleton picked clean by hawks, foxes, wolves and hyenas, that had stripped it down until nothing remained but stones and ragged thorns.

"What's your name?" Aunt Saliha asked.

"Muhammad."

"God's blessings on him. You'll stay here for two months, as a favor to the doctor, and your rent will be two hundred *riyals* a month."

I agreed to the terms, much to the doctor's pleasure. You'll leave his room now, and he'll be able to set back to a normal life again. He'll receive the sick at night, and won't have to apologize for making you wait outside.

The hawk was a distant speck, spiraling higher and higher until it entered the sun's orbit. You followed it until it disappeared and your eyes hurt from staring at the magnitude of light.

"There's only one condition," Aunt Saliha said, "and that's you keep the room clean. Ustadh Walid never swept his room once in five years, his dirtiness helped turn my hair white. And you may as well know that I forbid the use of radios."

"There's no cause for worry," I said, "I don't have a radio." I realized later she was so deaf she wouldn't have heard even if I'd played al-Qahim's songs!

"Hurry up then," she said, "before it starts getting hotter."

You laughed, something you hadn't done for so long that it hurt.

"But is there still one stone left unkindled by the sun?" you asked.

With the movement of the sun towards the western chain of mountains, you were aware of the passing of time. During the six interminable days that had passed, you'd tried to acquaint yourself with small details of life covered in dust. Nothing came clear, and those things you remembered seemed inseparable from some inscrutable dream. You could do nothing to retrieve this loss; those days were burnt-out, expended embers. The hopeless sorrow had penetrated your body; it shook violently like a bird with clipped wings. You thought your head was going to explode into molten lava, so you cupped it heavily, feeling the perspiration stream down your wrists.

"Muhammad," you said to yourself, "remember what the doctor said."

"And what did he say?"

"That the best way to kill time here is to sleep. If you can't kill time, it will kill you."

Ustadh Muhammad laughed until he felt a thread of blood stand out in his neck. You shouted, "Why did you insist on remaining fully awake, then? Why?"

You resolved to try and sleep, but memories and the heat of the sandy floor intensified your alertness. With difficulty you got to your feet, shook your head, and felt the arid things of the past begin to crack. An entire year crawled slowly through your limbs.

8

Silence maintained an equilibrium in the room, a still that was so intense it emitted a whistle—a high-pitched resonance that was bearable at first, and afterwards impossible. Silence is symbolic of a vast desert which you had to cross before death got you through thirst or isolation.

The walls, the bats, the greenfinches, the monkeys, the hawks and the crawling white ants, all of them formed part of the gelatinously composite body of silence.

A sharp sound crossed the room, eating up the air, the ceiling, and causing you to tremble. The desert makes for vulnerability, a crossing between life and death accompanied by fever and burning limbs. You're unarmed, pursued, and that mosquito, it too can grow to be the size of the desert.

You placed your head between your feet and wrapped your arms around your knees. When the wind grew louder than the mosquito, you began to roll in front of it like a dry straw.

You didn't even have the time to look behind, or overhead, to sense the huge wings that filled the horizon. You hid in the sands. Your fingers started to dig down, and when your perspiration mixed with the sand it formed a sort of paste. You tried to locate your cells, but withdrew, baffled by the alienation of things and the impossibility of escaping death. Then a sound arrested your attention, one that seemed as remote as your childhood. You looked up from between your knees and saw a man ploughing the waste: it was Abu Muhammad.

How can such a good man survive this desolation? you wondered. It seemed impossible that Abu Muhammad should put his plough's iron wings to the test in the heart of the wilderness. Nothing could take in such unmitigated sterility of earth.

It became less easy to distinguish how you met. The phenomenon of forgetting faces, of time seeming to fly, had become a part of your identity. It's like being one of the living dead; a revenant who exists between a nightmare and an even crueller awakening. You're the propounder of the kingdom of non-existence, a narrator of anticipated stories, the occupant of a life about to be extinguished, and of a death about to generate life to everything here from the white ant to the summits of Aseer.

You can't recollect the conditions of your first meeting, nor the portentous hour that witnessed it, sprung from the noon as from the mouth of a volcano. He was screaming,

screaming with all the power left to him, and with his thin body he was trying to break the circle that trapped him, while words and the physical presence of others suggested he impose some control on his hysteria. At that moment Ahmad Lufti was dangerously close to the fingers that would have strangled him, and leaning back icily against a stone wall. "If only my hands could reach you, I'd break your neck, or rather I'd throw you to the crows."

Ahmad Lufti smiled again: "If you want the house, you must pay two hundred and fifty *riyals* every month. Otherwise you won't be allowed across the threshold."

Fatima took refuge in Abu Abd al-Rahman's house. She cried at first, then tried to go out, but many hands restrained her from doing so.

"You can't go out," they told her. "Men will solve this problem. I had instructed Abu Abd al-Rahman not to rent this room to anyone, but he was afraid you'd all go to another village this year. There was nothing I could do. You know the rent's invaluable to us."

Ahmad Lufti was leaning back against the wall. What kind of wall is it that's disposed to keep him erect? If someone else had acted as he did, they would have been hit by a thunderbolt.

Everyone knows where Ahmad Lufti comes from, but what sort of wall is this that protects him from falling?

It's rumored that he got married here. The girl was a good peasant from one of those villages eroded by hunger and baked by the implacable severity of drought. He stayed with his bride for two months. Jabir, the head of police and his loyal friend, claimed Ahmad Lufti was two months trying to consummate the marriage but failed.

70

Jabir laughs at the thought.

"Imagine! Two whole months and he couldn't do anything." He laughs again: "I think I could have penetrated one of the slopes of the Aseer mountains in that time!" Laughter reverberates.

"When are you going home, Ustadh Ahmad?"

"Probably at the end of this year. I've had enough."

He used to say this casually, as though he had no responsibilities except eating his fill and waiting for the end of the year.

"Have you packed your cases?"

"No," he'd say. "I can't return just yet. I'll wait until next year."

It was always like this.

"And what about your bride? What will become of her? Go back to her and consummate your marriage."

And once, when wine had intoxicated him, Jabir said: "Why don't you let me do the thing for you?"

Ahmad Lufti realized the thunderbolt that had been aimed at him, despite Jabir's attempts to pass the incident off as a joke. He sat and cried despite the other's attempt to comfort him like a child. By the next evening Ahmad Lufti was sneaking to Hanash the baker's shack, for the latter spends every Friday night in al-Qunfudhah.

With the assistance of his foot, Abu Muhammad sank the plough deep into the dry earth. The ox turned a half circle and returned. The desert's too vast. Who has the strength to plough it? Who can grow a single rose in it? Yes, all right, a rose would be impossible, but who could even create just a little shade?

This is his second year here, in the desert's implacable desolation. He came last year, looked at Sabt Shimran, and muttered something incomprehensible. There wasn't even anyone to whom he could address himself.

"Are we going to live here . . . in this village?"

"Yes . . . right here."

"But that's impossible!"

"This is one of the best villages in the al-Qunfudhah region. You must thank God you stumbled on this village. But no, maybe it's your daughter's luck, maybe it's hers."

But Fatima said nothing. Since coming here, and being enveloped by a landscape that induces alienation, she said nothing. She realized that her only protection was to envelop herself in the dark of this desolate night that moved around her. She lived in its inner recesses, her mind mapped out by the winds. This was the most she could do in order to remain true to herself. The desert's huge; the plough bites into the ground.

At first a small soft hand stretched to Fatima's breast. Her body shook, but didn't resist that alien contact. Then a different hand seemed to telescope from the first one, then a rougher hand reached for her breast and Fatima fidgeted, drew away a little, but there was no hiding place. The darkness closed in; a black viscous liquid covered her body. She tried to stand up, but couldn't find her feet . . . she screamed, but the chains around her feet became so tight she went numb. She tried to scream, but the hands had drawn so near they threatened to reach inside her, destroy her equilibrium, her memory, her dream, and her still unevolved future.

She crouched in the corner, her eyes blown up huge with terror, her lip trembling, her hands restlessly sifting through sand. A cloak covered her animal terror.

A hand returned to her breast, moulding its contour,

72

before another tightened its grip, and still another raised her dress and slipped in to find the other breast. Fatima waved her arm like someone asleep who's trying to chase away a snake that's intruded into her dream.

She looked for an exit, but the door receded. The walls advanced on her, while hundreds of hands pursued her retreating figure. There was no refuge other than inside her beleaguered body, and no shield against the attack short of disowning a physical presence. There were so many different hands—a soft, a rough, a chapped one, scores of them lacerating her breasts, tipping her into a vertiginous whirlpool, a storm that left her hanging in an intermediary state between heaven and earth. Her footsteps were diminished by the enormity of the space in which she found herself.

"Father . . ."

"What is it, Fatima?"

"Nothing, nothing, Father, nothing at all."

"If only we could plant vegetables here. Something, anything. Isn't it possible to do something with the soil? We have an abundance of water, the fault's with the land. It's true water's the great life-giver, but how will it ever impart a green vegetation to this earth?"

"Father, you can at least try."

"The one person who could help us is Abu Abd al-Rahman. He has a piece of land near the well. If he'd agree to my working it, I'd begin immediately."

Abu Abd al-Rahman agreed, but that wasn't sufficient to impart fertility to the earth.

Beads of sweat gathered on his forehead and dripped on to the points of his mustache. They burnt in like a bee's sting. He rubbed them off with the back of his hand,

and the green and white striped shirt glued to his back absorbed the rest.

Sixty years old ... and you've nothing better to show than this land with its resistant thorns. The plough bit into the earth, and once again the ox turned a half circle, then returned. The sun described its implacable cycle without caring for Abu Muhammad's good intentions. If there'd once been hope in his dust-filmed eyes then it had disappeared. Hope?

It's possible Abu Muhammad realized the futility of his task, long before the ox completed its tenth round. He must have realized what he was doing would change nothing, that sand can't be converted into arable land. But he had to go on in order to convince himself of the challenge of being.

"This land defeats me, Fatima."

> It defeats me.
> It betrays my sweat
> my plough.
> It deceives these two hands
> destroys my longing for life.
> It betrays me.

And in that silent wilderness stretching to the limits of space, sand propagated sand. It was from there that a voice questioned,

"Abu Muhammad, what hope have you got now? Two whole months have passed, months of misexpended labor. Your water hasn't quickened the earth, your obstinacy in trying to turn sand into soil has gone unrewarded."

"I shan't pay another *fils* even if I'm forced to sleep out in the open with foxes and wolves."

"That's your right," said Ahmad Lufti. "I'm not forcing you to rent this room."

Abu Muhammad shook violently, kicking up the burning embers of his anger.

"Death's the only thing you deserve," he said, and charged towards him.

Abu Abd al-Rahman, who was up till now trying to stand between Abu Muhammad and Ahmad Lufti, suddenly charged himself, shouting:

"I'm the one who'll drink your blood, you bastard."

Ahmad Lufti retreated until he was back up against the wall. Men approached him, anger expressed in their fists and in the raised sticks with which they were armed.

But Jabir appeared suddenly. "No-one will touch him so long as I live," he shouted. "Get back, the lot of you."

This wasn't the first time he'd been known to intervene and save him. Abu Muhammad appeared to mirror all that was most beautiful in man, and to generate a spontaneous, country generosity, characteristics that were unknown to Ahmad Lufti.

Oh, desert. The sun's gold nugget is indomitable.

The incident, happening as it did in a small village, grew to be a major scandal in the teaching community. It reverberated through future generations.

You trip over again. The dark sand burns—it's desolate, like the bats' eyes, and sharp to the touch as the beaks of greenfinches. Fatima huddled in a dark corner of Abu Abd al-Rahman's house, trying to collect herself, trying to imagine a plausible escape from all this destruction. Her body felt estranged, it was being scooped into a vacuum like a huge mouth sucking at a rod of sugar cane.

Abu Muhammad didn't take his old lodgings at Abu Abd al-Rahman's house. He rushed away shouting at the top of his voice, "Fatima!" Then he turned to Ahmad Lufti and said, "Even if we have to sleep out in this wilderness we will, just to show you we won't be pawns to your greed."

Fatima pulled her body away from ravaging hands. She'd dried up completely. She maneuvered her body away as a sign of exhaustion. She had no defense between her body and the persistence of those hands.

And there, in the middle of a field overtaken by the desert, Abu Muhammad lay down with Fatima beside him, and both slept. One night they woke up to find the world darker than usual. They felt around them and discovered the presence of walls and a door through which light seeped, together with the howling of wolves, and the inquisitive eyes of foxes. They knew then that they had a room, something like a small cell, exiled at the end of the world, and belonging to Abu Abd al-Rahman. It had been a store-room for corn, and inhabited by snakes and rats, and now in its state of disintegration fit only for those who wished to hide away, for those who kept their eyes open and fixed on terror. May its desolation flower!

9

The cock crowed, for the first time in two years. It kept on until the cactus opened and the stones in the valley began fidgeting, and the hills cradled their heads on the mountain slopes. The foxes were roused by it; they sensed its presence as potential prey.

The cock crowed.

That meant that there were people in the neighborhood who should wake up. Isn't that true, Muhammad? It's a necessary stimulus after you've almost dug a hole and thrown your body into it to await the winds to cover you with sand or the arrival of a thunderbolt.

It crowed, perched on the dry tree trunk that was its home, and facing a window as wide as the horizon. The dark hen fluttered its wings. Nothing seemed worthy of this chanticleer. It put its head under its wings and went back to sleep.

The white hen didn't move. It was like a stone, dead but alert in the desert. It couldn't bend its legs properly. It was very tall, an oddity, like a cross between a pelican and an ordinary chicken.

Mu'ida's voice traveled across space as though it had evolved from a dream. It was like a bullet searching for a body to hit. The bleating of her sheep filled the air. Despite the presence of two lifelike scarecrows, thousands of greenfinches invaded the thousands of white corn cobs, voracious to clean the crop.

Mu'ida beat her empty tin can, but the birds didn't move. She waded out into the field and beat her can again. Even when she motioned with her arms the birds didn't take fright. She shivered, ran, and finally escaped with her sheep. From the distance came the echo of rifles. The birds scattered, their craws crammed, stained with the blood of those who'd been shot, and moved on to a different part of the field.

For a moment you might have believed that Mu'ida was stealing looks at you through the bars of the window, despite her father's admonitions that she stay away from the homes of the teachers.

"Stay away, Mu'ida, you're only twelve years old, stay away before you get burned. I know that nothing gives you more pleasure than to spy on the Ustadh, you little rascal. But I've nothing to offer, so stay away."

The red-bottomed monkeys sat on the burning rocks and watched. Their young clung to their mother's backs, anxiously taking in the crack of bullets, watching the live and the dead birds, waiting for the unexpected to happen. They remained there, unmoving, for hours. The rocks would have scorched a human hand. There was nothing to eat but corn, and the landscape was one of monotonous stones and thorn.

As gun fire reverberated, so flocks of greenfinches gusted into the air, while the more daring remained unperturbed, balanced on the stalks and worked at the life-source with their beaks.

The monkeys lacked their agility. Haj Saud had often laughed at their dormancy, but today he was silent. The monkeys swiveled their necks, climbed the mountain slopes and disappeared. What followed was their screams. The wolves were also searching for food.

You crossed the road, that same road which stretched between the neglected room on the outskirts of the village and the school gate. The doom palm trees spread behind the room; there's a little slope a short distance away, beyond that a growth of wild thorns, a short, tortuously narrow road, then the valley where you see tire-treads, and the imprints of cattle and sheep.

What you feared wasn't the burning noon which began before dawn, but that someone would ask you about Ustadh Muhammad. You knew questions would be fired at you before you even had time to reach the school gate.

"We don't see you with Ustadh Muhammad today. We hope there is nothing wrong?"

You feared just that, and so took a detour on your way to the dense thorn bushes. No one was there and yet you had the feeling you were watched. The road seemed full of people, full of questions.

It was tiring, picking your way through the thorns with their spiked armor, until you came out on the road and resumed your usual pace.

Shaikh Hajar passed in his jeep . . . He slowed to say

good morning. He's the school proprietor, the shaikh who presides at the mosque and the husband of four women who are said to be the most beautiful in Thuraiban.

He enquired about your health and affairs, and spoke of the advantages to be gained by having a motorcycle.

"You need a motorcycle, Ustadh. It's a good distance from your house to the village."

He went on to enquire of your relations with Haj Saud, and to assure you of the latter's authenticity both as a landlord and as a person; but all the time you felt he wanted you to contradict him, so he could curse Saud to hell.

The suspicion in your eyes portrayed how you were waiting for the course of the conversation to change. It seemed as though the whole world's questions were lurking among the trees, waiting for the right moment to pounce on you. But nothing of the sort happened. The questions remained hidden and you continued on your way.

No sooner had you parted from Shaikh Hajar than you found yourself approaching the well where Salim al-Shimrani, who was back on leave from the army, had herded his sheep. You would rather have avoided him, given your aversion to soldiers and the police, and the disquieting effect they had on your chemistry.

Despite your efforts to deflect his scrutiny, he looked at you with a discerning eye. "You're pale, Ustadh, you've lost a lot of weight."

"Why do you ask that, Salim? I'm fine, as you can see. I have all my health and strength."

You trembled, panic was attacking your nerves. You said to yourself, "It had to happen!"

"You should rest, Ustadh. I'm going to be around for a month, taking refuge from the Tabuk heat."

"And how am I supposed to rest in this blazing climate?" you asked.

He didn't answer. You could see the village in the distance, its white houses contrasted with the dark shade of its high stone walls, and its towers looking skywards as though officiating over a tribal war.

Voices reached you from the village square; and an odor of cattle dung was carried down-wind.

For a brief moment you were overcome by the burning conviction you should return home, and so avoid those incessant questions that had you sit up sleepless at night, shaking with fever. If he's disappeared, then let him enjoy his freedom.

You stopped at the entrance to the village, a narrow passage marked by a huge round stone on one side and a dung-hill on the other. If Shaikh Hajar and Salim al-Shimrani had avoided the question, you felt sure that the school principal wouldn't. You stood at the door of the administrative room—ceiling, walls and straw, and they said, "This is the school."

"This?" you asked.

"That's right," they answered.

"But where will the students sit?"

"They'll have to sit on blankets until the benches arrive. The blackboards should be here in a few days."

"But there's lots of houses in the village which would lend themselves to a school," you argued.

Haj Saud bent in your direction and said, "But Shaikh Hajar's beaten us to them."

"How?" you asked.

81

"By killing two sheep for the director of education, and by inviting Aunt Saliha and her daughter Salima to his house, and by sitting up with him until dawn."

"But what's their relationship?" you asked.

"Don't you find Salima beautiful?" he enquired.

"Yes, I suppose so."

"And undoubtedly hot blooded like her mother," he added.

"How do you know?" you asked.

"They say Aunt Saliha isn't like any other woman. She has two clitorises!"

Voices reached you from every direction, dissonant, clamorous, creating a confused hubbub.

"You're late today, Ustadh."

"And you're particularly early," you answered.

"This is the first time you've been late . . . I hope there's nothing wrong?"

"Of course not," you said.

You imagined your depressed features would indicate your state of mind. Instead you scribbled your signature on the page of the office register, crossed an imaginary threshold and said, "Rabab Rami."

You began your lesson with Rami visiting Rabab's house.

"Are you married, Ustadh Muhammad?"

"No," you replied.

"Why don't you marry someone like Rabab, Ustadh?"

"Why, Aun?"

"So you can make love, Ustadh, make love!!"

He told you this as if you knew nothing about worldly affairs.

The students broke into mischievous laughter. You

82

struck the blackboard with your hand, until eventually an uneasy silence dominated the room, broken only by an occasional giggle. Aun, who was only seven years old, leant back against the dry straw wall, with the indifference of a spectator.

"Who's going to read?"

Rami visited Rabab's house . . . Two unbearable periods followed by an interminable third. The pressure closed in on you, your pulse accelerated, and you felt as though you were trying to break free from the earth's magnetic field.

But nobody asked about his absence. Was Ustadh Muhammad just a small insect who came and left without anyone noticing? Were they unappreciative of his qualities? He was a good, loving man with a touch of sadness, true, but he never hated anyone.

You approached the principal, who was deeply immersed in writing letters to the Department of Education. You scruffed him by the neck, lifted him as high as the gallows and screamed in his face:

"Why don't you ask? Why? Did Ustadh Muhammad mean so little to you?"

"Have you gone mad, Ustadh?"

You regained your senses and apologized.

The bell rang for the sixth period. You ran out before the students reached the school door. The sun hung in scarlet embers between the huge stone on one side and the dung-hill on the other. The heat was such you felt consumed by its center. You kept wondering why the police didn't apprehend you. Who'd forgotten who, and how? There'd been no intrusion on your privacy since yesterday evening. It seemed as though even the police had forgotten about Ustadh Muhammad. Perhaps the details you gave were lost on them—they must have been charred by the heat and were now gathering themselves for the cooler evening. They'd most likely forgotten about someone's disappearance, and forgotten too that they'd been ordered to chase me as far as the door of my room. Or could they have found him? That would be the worst thing of all. You discounted this possibility. He too never liked the police or the military. The worst that could happen would be for the police to track him.

I shouted, "Keep well hidden, the winds have come to you . . ." Salt poured out of your skin; it formed crystallized fountains in this scorching land. The void in front of you turned into thousands of mirrors, a blinding distortion that reflected your face. You stared into the mirror and asked:

"Have you seen Ustadh Muhammad? He's not with you today."

"Which Ustadh Muhammad?"

"There's only one, and he disappeared."

"Disappeared? I didn't hear of this."

You smashed the mirror into fragments with your fists and the hot blood hissed from your fingers. You felt no pain, only an increasing numbness. All that you could do was mark the difference between the thread of blood and the thread of perspiration . . . between sanguine viscosity and the coagulation of time.

The cock crowed again. But this time the cactus didn't respond, nor did the stones fidget. The foxes remained dormant, and even the brown hen failed to raise its head from the cover of its dark wing, and enquire as to what had provoked that call.

10

The impact of fists almost broke the door of the room into splintered fragments. They always come at the end of the night. They cross obscure passageways, unlimited distances. I've given them everything, and now there's nothing left to take. The desert stretches to the sea's edge, and I own almost nothing of it, a narrow area half the size of an airport, which contains thirty sacks of corn, two beds and a sandy table, and an unlimited proliferation of white ants, white to the point of madness.

What do they want now? Let them go away. Let them turn over every stone in the hope of finding him, or let them climb to the summits of mountains and search for him in the eyes of hawks and beneath crows' wings. They might find him there. Do they really want to instill in me the belief that I'm he?

It won't work.

Their renewed impact threatened to slat the door to firewood.

"What do you want?"

"We want you."

The cock woke up. The brown hen had grown tired of looking up from beneath its wings, while the white hen stared with closed eyes framing an expression of indescribable stupidity.

In a light so pale it seemed to have traveled from an unidentifiable star, you recognized the face of one of the policemen, and said to yourself, "Thank God!"

The officer's lips parted, while the two policemen whispered: "It's him . . . he hasn't changed since noon."

You stared into the policeman's face, the same one who'd chased you all day, but saw nothing. You drew near to him. He was very thin. It hurt you that his night was encroached on by the necessity of looking for Ustadh Muhammad. But secretly, you whispered to yourself, "The world's still a good place."

An interval of silence ensued, broken finally by the howling of a wolf on the rocky slopes of the mountain. The officer resumed shaking his head:

"Yes it's him alright, it must be him."

A sudden storm got hold of you. Your leaves shook, your throat went dry, your eyes were blown up huge.

Have they caught him, you wondered, or have they come to arrest me? You were torn between conflicting probabilities. The storm racked you again, stars in the distance shiveringly dispersed, and the eyes of foxes converged in a single beam.

It had been a hard day, but you'd learnt something

which you wouldn't otherwise have realized. It was something to do with identity.

Just imagine if I'd been Ustadh Muhammad, try to conceive of him as me. That isn't especially difficult. And what would happen to me if I knew no one ever asked after me except the police.

But the world's still a good place!

The wind returned. The cold stung you, you shook like a bird in the snow, you withdrew into yourself, feeling your warmth evaporate.

"We were going to arrest you, but Haj Saud insisted we join him for dinner, so we dropped the idea. We spoke a lot about you, about you and Ustadh Muhammad."

You tried to work out what Haj Saud could have said to change the mind of the police. He's a good man, and an act of goodwill's in keeping with his character, but what could he have said?

"That's OK," you said, "the important thing is that you came. You know, someone must ask in the end, someone has to, even if it's a policeman? But have you found him?"

"We've come to ask you, has he returned home?"

"No . . ."

"Do you think he will?"

You didn't know how to answer. How could you predict whether he'd return or not.

"No . . . he won't return!" you heard yourself say.

"Then you're aware that he's gone?"

"No . . . not at all."

"And why shouldn't he return?" asked one of the two policemen. You couldn't distinguish which of the two had spoken.

87

"He may return, but there again he may not," you said.

The officer shook his head and said: "It doesn't matter now."

"Then I assume you've found his corpse," you replied.

You were about to burst into tears when the officer said,

"No, he's not dead."

"Then why's the matter no longer significant?" you asked.

"Because we know he's still in the district. He's really here."

"He's really here? Why keep me in suspense when this is the news I've been waiting to hear."

"The important thing is that you're well and comfortable. The rest is our concern.

"Can you describe him to us accurately?" they continued. "That would help us a lot. And if you have a picture of him, then so much the better."

"He's about my height," you said, "and has brown curly hair like mine, brown eyes, wheat-blond skin and is of a melancholy disposition."

"Almost like you?" they said.

"Yes."

"And has the same name?"

"Yes, that's another coincidence."

"Are there other similarities with which we're not acquainted?"

"No."

"Where did you meet the first time?"

"I can't recall. Sometimes I can believe I've known him since childhood, but I can't be sure of this since he does nothing to familiarize my memory. His predominant

88

mood is one of silence, and incommunicativeness char-
acterizes our relationship. I'm sure he hides an unfathomable secret in his heart. It could have been that we
first met in Jeddah, no, in al-Qunfudhah, when we came
down from the jeep. We shook the dust from our clothes
and faces. He looked pale with fatigue. In those days I
could draw a clear picture of him, an image I was always
trying to get to know . . ."

"And the picture? Do you have a photograph of him?"

"No. I told you he looks like me. Do you want me to
give you my photograph?"

"How is it he both resembles you and has your name?"
He began shaking his head again.

"I told you. It's just a coincidence!"

"We'll see you tomorrow night, then."

"Why don't you come in and rest until the morning?"
you asked.

"We'll carry on looking for him," they replied.

"I'll come with you."

"No, look for him around the house."

"Try to be kind to him," you said.

"We assure you," they replied, "no harm will come to
him."

And before you could arrest your hand from its motion
of waving goodbye, they'd disappeared.

. . . .
. . . .

You stared at the sky. It was full of watery stars, and
then your eyes returned to the cock and the two hens.
The white hen was still frozen in its uncomprehending
inertia, while the brown hen had likewise remained static.
The cock momentarily shifted the position of its legs.

Before starting the search, you stepped back into the room. Your crossing the threshold opened up nights buried in the interior. Memories of nights spent inside and out and their endless multiplication of time and space.

Once again you tripped over the pot. You felt a sticky liquid on your feet. You said, "How many times have I told him to wash the pot!"

You felt the edge of the bed, the remains on the table, the table itself, the soft sand. It was by the suitcase; the flash-light you'd been searching for, and should have found much earlier. You kept a tight hold on it. It was the last of the night stars. The only constellation that lights up this room.

The circle of light began to move, a magic eye probing the dark that stretches to infinity. The eye was looking at you, flexing whenever you moved your hand, then steadying in its dilation.

A flurry of bats left the room; the one that remained behind stuck itself to the wooden ceiling.

The magic eye focused and moved in on it, hunted the bat to a corner of the room over the corn sacks, caught it in one convulsive movement as it soared and was swallowed by the dark.

Suddenly, you remembered Ustadh Muhammad. You hadn't really forgotten him anyway. You recalled the incessant war he waged with the bats, right up until the time he left. The nights are interminable here, and the desert incomparably desolate. There's nothing as forlorn and desolate as the desert. Time has the same broken meaning as the earth which hasn't known fertility for centuries. Both are smashed entities.

Ustadh Muhammad had tried desperately to fill the vacuum. He would follow the bats from one corner of the room to another, before stretching out on the bed and directing the flashlight towards whatever creatures of the night took refuge in hidden places of the room; a nocturnal game you'd almost forgotten.

When Ustadh Muhammad told you these creatures needed to get accustomed to the light, you laughed. "What's your interest in all this?" you'd ask.

"I don't know," he would reply, "only I believe there's a connection between us and them. Don't you see how we adopt their manner of staring at the dark."

"Then why don't you leave them in peace," I said.

But Ustadh Muhammad won't let the thing rest. He switches on the flashlight and the magic eye moves up the nearby wall, a little circle of light illuminating what it touches. It widens its radius as it touches on other walls. Then abruptly it gathers speed like a hawk. The bats move, fly off, stick to corners above our heads, but never leave the room.

Ustadh Muhammad puts out the flashlight again. He walks slowly over the soft sand in silence; the compacted darkness encompasses everything. When he reaches the furthest corner of the room, he raises his hand and fixes his eyes into abstract space. Then he throws a switch and the bats fly off. Only those half-lame with fatigue stay on before getting clear.

"The room should be closed for days with the light left burning at all times. That way the bats would grow accustomed to light and stay."

. . . .
. . . .

The foxes' eyes gleamed. The white hen seemed unable to get back to sleep, and the cock remained disinterested. The darkness increased until you could no longer discern the brown hen.

You too had circled round the room with the magic eye, penetrating the heart of darkness. You wondered if he could still be here, close to the house, and how did they know he was still in the neighborhood? You didn't know whether this was a good or a bad thing. He could be here or over there, and who was running away from who, and would the police catch up with you, they and silence, and time and the hungry greenfinches and the morose monkeys.

You went out into the night to the edge of the thorns and the doom palm trees. The foxes hurried away, and in the distance two eyes glowered like live coals. You tried to pick them out with the flashlight, but to no avail, and took big strides back to your room.

The bats had resumed their places in the corners. You could hear the fluttering of their wings around you, and their agitation increased your own feeling of apprehension. You didn't dare turn on the flashlight again for fear it would act as a nocturnal sun and attract all the solitary creatures of the wilderness. This was the first time you'd feared the light. You got up once or twice before throwing your head on the pillow and despite the suffocating heat you tented yourself in a woolen blanket, and pinpointed your eyes on a wide space in which the heat and cold of the world shared the cells of your body.

The bats swooped down in the direction of the flashlight. You held it firmly, but somehow it rolled away and switched itself on, causing you to duck under the blankets in fear. You clutched the covering with a tenacity fit to burst your blood-vessels. The light appeared to be tracking you, fixing its steady eye on your convulsed, rolling head.

Still clutching the blanket around you, you let your feet down on to the earthern floor. It was imperative to leave tonight.

Your first step was cautious, and you tripped on the second. A frenzy of wings beat the air, the volume of noise seeming to rise until it covered the whole world. You crawled towards the door, bumping your head against a concrete wall. The impact hurt as though you were discovering the wall for the first time. The circle of light followed you—and you went towards it like a moth that courts a flame. You had lost all sense of direction. Leather wings beat against you and you screamed. When the cock crowed their attack abated. They drew off as though startled by the arrival of the dawn. The ring of light continued to swing over the table, before it disappeared.

11

As the blade of the cleaver pierced the ground, so its wooden handle stood upright, as though an entanglement of roots deep in the sand had secured that fixity.

Suddenly, with the swiftness of an arrow, he rushed through the door, crossed the threshold, trembling, foaming, and came down with the cleaver on the ground.

It would have been possible that blood would have hissed from the particles of sand, but a kind of miracle happened.

He scrutinized the place with his small eyes, and with his emaciated face he exploded the noon.

"You won't stay here another minute, otherwise one of us will go to the grave."

You didn't understand anything of what was happening. Only that a face had drawn near you, its features lined from exposure to the desert, and fires blazing in its eyes. There was no explanation as to who it was or where it had come from.

"And why should we go?" you asked.

He looked at his shack, the one which stood out like a clown's hat and said: "My woman's there, my honor's being defiled here and now. How could Haj Saud agree to sell me for a hundred *riyals*? How?"

At that moment things came clear.

You said, "We rented this room from Haj Saud, so you can speak directly to him."

"You must go away before my blood boils," he replied. He bent to the ground and extracted the cleaver forcibly from its place, before his eyes returned to your features.

"You must go now."

Ustadh Muhammad wasn't there. Most likely he wasn't around at all, otherwise your answer would have been more daring.

"I can't tell you anything except to go and speak to Haj Saud. If he tells us to leave, then we'll leave."

At this, the man with the cleaver relented a little.

This was your second day at Thuraiban. Why didn't he come yesterday? And as if he was reading your thoughts, he said:

"I didn't know there were strangers living in front of my family's eyes. Otherwise no one would have slept in this room while I was alive."

Everything that was happening pointed to a bloody struggle, and the unpropitious omens of death-birds.

"I'll give you up to this evening. After that, no-one will stop me throwing you into the valley."

After saying this, he picked up his cleaver and left.

95

You stood there bewildered in the middle of the room. You must do something, you must talk to Haj Saud.

Red flames fanned out from the incandescent noon. Everything had gone into hiding. There wasn't a hawk in sight, the sand and stones shrunk from the glare, the trees, the shadows, the crows and sparrows had all disappeared. But are there really sparrows here?

When you called out Haj Saud appeared from one of the shacks outside of your field of vision. Five of them punctuated a small hill; there was a common threshing ground, some corn sacks, and two wives about whom you heard later, but never saw.

"What's up, Ustadh?"

You answered in the manner of someone who wishes to make a request to a Bedouin *shaikh*:

"When we live in your house, doesn't it follow that we're under your protection?"

"I'd protect you with my life."

"Then get that madman off our trail."

"Who?"

When I told him what had happened, he said: "So now we have Ghabshan to deal with. Leave him to me, Ustadh, I know how to deal with him."

. . . .

The emaciated Ghabshan made no further attempt to cross the threshold. He simply sat on a black rock in front of his shack, spanning the divide with his anger. Then he circled the building, drew near to the room, stopped in a state of suspended threat, and returned to his former position. He repeated this approach several times, advancing and coming to a halt, his suppressed anger checked by some invisible line stretching between our

96

door and his shack which it was taboo to cross. He seemed paralyzed by that invisible barrier.

"Ghabshan . . . Who's Ghabshan?"

You knew nothing about him. He was worn through to the skeleton, dry as a piece of wood, stooped like a roof about to collapse, his sixty years contained in a shriveled body. And try as you did to clarify things, there wasn't any easy way to explain what was happening. It's true you caught sight of a woman yesterday, but only her shadow wrapped in a cloak. You couldn't distinguish whether she was coming or going, and you were still debating her intentions when she disappeared inside the shack and never showed again. But it still wasn't clear what had provoked this anger.

You said, "There's a woman, Ustadh Muhammad."

"It's not a human being," he replied. "It's a cloak. All you see is a black tent moving."

"I see a black cloak moving," you said.

"And you can't be sure of what's inside it."

Everything ended and began with this. A cleaver embedded in the ground, its handle upright, smooth like a snake. And a man foaming in the middle of the room.

Evening came, then the sun rose again, and blazed, and was extinguished, and a new morning appeared, and a new night. And still Ghabshan threatened to close that narrow gap between the cleaver blade and the shedding of blood. Still he hovered between his shack and the store room.

You said, "Ustadh Muhammad, I think we should tell the police."

This was the first time you'd conceived of this option.

"No, . . . don't worry," he said, "he won't do anything.

97

Have you spoken to Haj Saud?"

"Yes."

"And did he promise you anything?"

"That no harm will come to us."

"Then relax. If Ghabshan was intent on doing something, he would have done it by now."

But you couldn't rid your mind of his image; a man approaching only to return. Even after you'd locked the door and gone to bed, your fear persisted.

You reassured yourself that Haj Saud's word possessed irrefutable power. It was his word that stood as a divisive line between the cleaver blade and blood.

Two days later, you discovered the presence of bats in the room. They occupied half of it, hidden by corn sacks, their heads pointing downwards, while their claws held to the wood. You'd heard of the notorious blood-sucking bats. True to their name of vampire bats they'd suck blood from a sleeper's outstretched foot, and retreat without his so much as waking. You wielded a large stick and rushed into the dark interior of the room. The bats fled. You drew back, you closed the windows and secured the door and went to bed.

As though to comfort you, Ustadh Muhammad said, "There aren't any vampire bats in this country." But you still took the precaution of swaddling yourself in blankets.

When you got up the next day, and before you had time to open the door, the bats were already zigzagging from one corner of the room to another. You were terrified as you pointed to them.

"Look! How did they manage to enter . . . How?"

"Through there," observed Ustadh Muhammad, pointing to a small hole in the wall. You hurried and blocked it with a large stone, packing it into place with smaller ones.

Haj Saud said, "Ustadh, Ghabshan's a good man, and remember this is the first time a schoolteacher's come to the village. You should make allowances for him. He's over sixty and has a beautiful woman. He's jealous to the point of possession."

"But we won't eat her up!" you replied.

He said, "I've spoken to him and warned him. He won't be able to harm anyone."

But Ghabshan, whom you hadn't seen on your immediate arrival, was still circling round and round the shack, like an African dancing around a fire, tense, overstrained, foaming at the mouth, the evil blazing in his eyes and communicating itself to the stones. After deliberating, he seemed suddenly to have found a solution to his dilemma.

A jeep drew up. A woman approaching sixty climbed down, evidently exhausted, her back so stooped it looked broken, her complexion blackened from age and exposure. She carried a stick in her hand.

She looked towards you, and towards the room. She muttered some imprecation you couldn't hear. A few moments later, a cloaked woman came out of the shack. She climbed into the rear of the jeep, while Ghabshan took up a position next to the driver. The jeep roared off in a cloud of dust.

"What's happened, Haj Saud?"

"Ghabshan has brought his old wife, Aunt Jarada, here, and taken his new wife to the village."

"But can Aunt Jarada endure staying here all by herself?"

"Ghabshan comes here before dawn and goes to the corn field, then returns before sunrise to the village. He brings Aunt Jarada provisions, then goes off again."

"So Ghabshan's run away with his young wife," you told Ustadh Muhammad, "and brought the old one here to this wilderness?"

The next night you took the same precautions against exposing your body while asleep. You couldn't bear the thought of bats sucking blood from your toes, and then flying off without your feeling anything!

They say they leave almost indiscernible wounds. They perform the act rapidly and disappear before the pain registers.

You bolted the door again.

"Why don't you try and relax," said Ustadh Muhammad. "Ghabshan won't be able to harm us."

"But I'm afraid of the bats. They could kill us in the night by sipping our blood."

You can't recall how long it took you to realize those bats belonged to another species, and when you adopted a rational means of interacting with them, Ustadh Muhammad had by then assumed another line of approach.

12

In a world devoid of all surprise and expectation, devoid of any joy, the glory of Saad's daughter increased. Her only rival was Aunt Saliha's daughter. In the permanently dark, stone-walled grocery with its narrow entrance door, Saad's daughter exercised her charms on both stone and men.

There she'd hold sway, but her fruits were always expensive, unmarked by human hand. Her voice excited like the undulation of a waist burning with desire. She'd go deep into the recesses of the shop as though the earth had swallowed her. Now near, and now far, she appeared inaccessible, an illusion or a nightmare that concentrates itself in an empty spot, a fathomless abyss, or else she steps out of a cactus forest, soft, wounding, and no hand dares to touch her.

She'd take shelter in that recess, her voluptuous body always out of reach, her body untouched by anyone except Ustadh Waleed, if we're to believe the rumor. But who can stay here seven years for Saad's daughter?

Ustadh Waleed set out on a long journey this year, and they say she cried when someone secretly told her he wouldn't be returning for another year. That was the only time Saad's daughter lost control of herself and her father's shop. She ran. But Ustadh Waleed had discovered seven years was too long to wait. During that time he'd revolved around her, and when he finally caught hold of her it was not before he'd begun to write letters to himself.

He used to go up to Baljarashi and project them down in the direction of Sabt Shimran. The letters would come down from the heights of Aseer and be caught up in the accelerating race of flood water.

Ustadh Waleed used to watch the floods for his ship, and for the world which he'd left behind seven years ago. He'd run towards the mail, where water and desert meet, open his letter and return with an air of jubilation.

The thought of Saad's daughter was no longer sufficient comfort. The desert didn't rise above the solitude of its sands. It remained there, lurking in desolate corners, consigned to oblivion. But already rumors were abroad. People had the suspicion that Ustadh Waleed was in love with Saad's daughter, and that driven to distraction by love, he went every week in the direction of Baljarashi.

"Where are you going, Ustadh Waleed?"

"To Baljarashi to visit my brother and some friends."

But everyone knew those friends would run away in

time. They'd collect their torn limbs and jostle each other running through the dark nights in the direction of light, any light that showed up. Some of them would fall down, and the crows would prey on them, returning them north, wrapped in their wings, their voices a hoarse outcry. And some of them would struggle with death until life exploded in their veins. Then they'd gather together their remains and disappear.

There, in that corner of the world called Sabt Shimran, Ustadh Waleed would huddle down, trying to savor his last good days with Saad's daughter; but for a long time that had proved an inadequate diversion.

Saad's daughter ran but the desert was larger than her body. She ran, but Ustadh Waleed, who'd almost, one dark night, decided to stay forever, left his body and projected into the wilderness, where he was never found.

Saad's daughter ran in the direction of every bird that soared, expecting to find his body. But the eagles and ragged crows would rush in her direction, beating their wings, and she'd smell in them the odor of blood and follow their flight-path. But it was already late; time had opened up huge gulfs.

Saad's daughter withdrew. It was said no one saw her again after that terrible year, and that she grew old and wrinkled, her stiffness pronouncing her decrepitude. But her voice remained youthful, for she was always calling for Ustadh Waleed, her lover.

Some said Saad's daughter was over a hundred years old, and that even when Ustadh Waleed was here, she was an old woman, and when he saw her he abandoned his body and was never seen again.

You were hesitant at first. You were about to step

103

towards the corner from where the voice issued, kindled, resonated, but you lacked courage to unravel this secret.

Ustadh Muhammad told you whoever touches her disappears. "You must stay away," he said. Then he laughed loudly. Ustadh Muhammad himself disappeared, and you knew, without having to verify it, that he'd never even entered Saad's daughter's grocery, or browsed through that darkness.

Saad would enter the shop and find her there among the sacks of rice and sugar and the cans of processed food. She'd draw sufficiently close to touch Pluto's shoulder with her palm, he who'd come from Milan, or the hand of one of the school teachers, then retreat a little. And Saad would smile and go into an adjoining room as though he was one of the ancients.

You said, "Pluto, you teach me Italian and I'll teach you Arabic."

He shook his head.

We'd already smashed the English language out of all recognition.

The paved road had already reached Sabt Shimran. Someone pointed it out saying: "It will go on from here." It had seemed impossible at the beginning.

For two years the Italians had been paving the desert to reach al-Qunfudhah. As for us, we used to reach it in a night and a half. Two years of labor to devise a road that would get them there in six hours! And why should anyone want to contract time to arrive there that quickly.

"But the moment a proper road reaches us, our entire lifestyle here will change," said Shaikh Hajar.

"I can't see any reason for opening a road here," Ahmad Lufti pronounced.

"We'll be a part of the world then," the teachers responded.

Fatima remained silent.

"Ustadh Muhammad," I said, "they say the road works have reached the village of Namira."

"Why should you be happy about that?" he asked. "There'll be a road, but the only time you'll use it is once when you enter that hell, and once when you leave it."

The Italians tried, without success, to find something in the landscape that corresponded to themselves. The desert was vast. At first they'd confronted it with a sense of wonder, expectant of some gain. They were fascinated by its gold face. When the sun rose they'd rush towards it, throwing sand at each other, as though they were running across a beach. And in the evening, preoccupied with the shadows skirting the edge of the dunes, they'd run again. And there in that desolate wilderness they'd hear the voice of Saad's daughter, burning with desire, and they'd rush towards her. Unable to define the source of that voice, they hurried in all directions. Some of them ran south to the borders of Yemen, while others continued east, brought up short only by their colliding with the Aseer mountains. Then there were bloody floods and detonations of thunder rocked the center of the world.

Although their company attempted to provide them with everything from matches to whisky, the alcohol-free beer they consumed took on a special flavor when they neared Saad's daughter. She moved elusively through them like a magic bird, her hair brushed with perfume and crowned with basil leaves. But no one saw her face.

"Pluto," I said, "do you believe the girl's a hundred years old? Anyhow, that's what they say." And I went on to tell him everything I'd heard about her.

"You're crazy," he said. "You're like the rest of your race—mad! Nothing fascinates you more than improbable tales."

"But Pluto," I said, "the age of legends is a thing of the past."

"That's what you think," he answered.

When we stood at the door of the grocery, her voice was unashamedly provocative. Pluto looked at me and said: "You're mad. Such a voice can only belong to a voluptuous woman, a real woman, full of desire."

But who was it who dared to hold her hand? Antonio? Or Ustadh Fathi who came looking for her from Namira?

Who was it who dared to touch her hand?

Suddenly the world spun out of orbit around him.

The voice shrilled, and the wilderness was full of it. Every creature took cover from that scandalous outrage. Thunder slammed across the skies and the floods followed. Saad came, he bellowed and swore, although his voice remained inaudible. Then a calm settled over the night, as if a beneficent dream had penetrated it, so that it became a night like any other in the world, clear and peaceful, speaking of a promised assurance. It grew quiet until you could almost believe you were dreaming in a room open to the world, and looking out on to an ordinary narrow street that was not without innocence in a place where a person might actually smile.

Perhaps the cold had seeped through to you from the room's sandy floor. You'd forgotten even the white ants, and were about to forget the storm. That moment of peace enveloped you with multi-colored birds and lyric songs. You fidgeted and turned over again, drawing the blanket up to your head. You huddled into yourself, placing your head near your knees. Saad's daughter seemed to you now like an amorphous nightmare that eluded clearly articulated features.

Why doesn't life retain this equipoise? you questioned. Why does it cut through all this with hawks and green-finches and storms, the enigma of Saad's daughter, the proliferation of white ants?

You threw off the blanket, sat up, and found yourself on the floor. You stretched out your hand to touch the sand. You stood upright and took a decisive step forward. When you relocated the bed, you lay on your back looking up at the ceiling, but couldn't see the bats. You tried to find the flashlight but it wasn't within reach. You didn't know how long you'd been asleep on the sandy floor.

I used to tell Ustadh Muhammad that white ants could be prevented from climbing the bed posts, by placing the legs in empty bean cans. The ants couldn't perform the feat of climbing up the can, down its inner side, and then up the bed's legs.

Haj Saud said, "If you put gasoline or oil inside the can, they'll never reach you."

It took courage to place your feet on the ground before reaching for the oil-container or the gasoline tank. You found yourself jumping, and a bat scuttered away. Your hand fumbled in the corner . . . here's the pot, there's the stove . . . but the oil and gasoline containers had dis-appeared. You tried to remember the last time you and Ustadh Muhammad had filled the stove with gasoline, or the last time you used the oil. You tried, but . . .

A voice reached you out of nowhere, its tone not entirely unfamiliar. Its tonality was fragile at first, but you were compelled to listen. You wanted to ascertain the precise location of that voice. It wasn't from Thuraiban, and then you realized the motorcycles were coming from the direction of Sabt Shimran. You were frightened and on the verge of going outside, before you remembered you risked being seen. You revolved around yourself, once, twice, you fell down, stood up, and returned to the window. You shook the bars, rattled them until blood streamed down your fingers.

"I told them to keep away," you shouted. "I told them that . . . and they promised me."

"You're witnesses to that, you're my witnesses," you screamed at the ceiling, pointing to the bats.

The noise approached, zoomed alongside the house, but didn't climb the little hill. Instead, the drone continued its forward thrust, accelerating away into the distance.

You took comfort in the thought that perhaps they'd missed the road. And although it was almost dawn and the light would assist them in finding you, you wished the morning would come.

"Why's the light so delayed?" you shouted.

Pluto had said, "Do you think we'll be allowed to cross the threshold?" There wasn't any distance between you and Saad's daughter.

"Pluto," you said, "where have you come from?"

"Milan," he replied.

"All the way from Milan?" you exclaimed with astonishment.

But perhaps he didn't understand you, and maybe you failed to register your surprise in an interpretable language.

108

A human explosion had occurred. Everything reverted to its opposite. At first they rushed, jostling each other, in the direction of Saad's grocery, and Saad took everything. As for them, they never arrived.

"Will you come with us today?" asked Pluto.

"Where are we going?"

"It doesn't matter," he said, "will you come?"

"Yes," you replied. Every journey carried with it the force of a hammer that broke the sharpness of time.

The Italians gathered in the wide squre in front of their camp. They looked at each other, then ran towards the cars. You ran too, bewildered.

Scores of motors roared into collective action and dispersed in different directions. Something was going on in the Italians' heads; they were ablaze with energy.

The cars stopped and the Italians stood in a circle. The cattle started off; instinct told them something was wrong, that a plan was being hatched against them. As the men closed in on them, they tried to find a break in the approaching human circle. The men were trying not to alarm them, but terror showed in their big eyes, their necks . . .

The cows were preparing to stampede, and then no one would be able to catch them. They'd lived here a long time, unintruded on, so could only panic at the white alien faces that came towards them, eyes shining with latent madness. The animals raised their heads and formed a protective mass. The human circle narrowed, and the beasts knew they were trapped. When the white hands started brandishing ropes, they packed tighter. This was all they could do. It was their only means of self-defense.

Suddenly the ropes twitched in the air but went wide of their intended aim. They lashed out again. This time the cows moved in fright and were about to disperse; but they regrouped in the middle of the contracting human circle. They reared and attempted to bolt, but everything closed in on them, space, the desert, while the mountains crowded them and almost blocked the flow of the valley.

The Italians drove the cattle towards the cars, and five or six of the herd huddled there alone. They were realizing an end to the wilderness, to the freedom that had comprised their way of life.

The engines roared into action again.

And there, behind the wide square, bulldozers had prepared a gaping wide hole, something like a communal burial ground. The men and cattle alighted and you stood there bewildered.

The Italian laborers rushed forward. "Come on!" Pluto shouted to you, a note of exhiliration in his voice.

There was a rapid exchange of laughter as they ran their hands over the cows' wombs.

They they broke down and cried.

The voice of Saad's daughter could be heard again in the distance. They trembled, they ran with half raised parts in the direction of the voice. They stormed on . . .

Some were running to the east, some to the west and some to the north. And the voice was setting the desert on fire.

13

When the Italian company working on paving the road from Jeddah down to Mahayil, south of al-Qunfudhah, first appeared with its chain of machinery, the people of Sabt Shimran, Thuraiban, Naqmah and al-Sawad rushed out, each holding the edges of his gown between his teeth. Women, children, old people and slim waisted young girls, all ravaged by tuberculosis, assembled, and the ensuing discussion wasn't unlike a debate in the Tihama valleys which descend from the heights of the Aseer mountains to the foot of the Red Sea. The intensity of speech is like that of the consuming climate—a scorching, arid torture, a parched desiccation that deprives everything of a protective shadow.

Over the months the road had written itself into local conversation. Not one assembly or gathering was held without the subject of the road assuming importance. It also formed the substance of those raw exchanges of talk made by the education inspectors who pounced on the villages morning and evening, leaving behind them pleasant words recorded in the schools' registers, and the skeletons of sheep slaughtered in honor of the visit, stripped completely of their meat.

It was hard to know why the road had acquired such significance. It had come to occupy the physical space of the desert and the mental space of the inhabitants and the teachers who'd come from the north. It had assumed priority over even the most painful events, and when a snake bit the Egyptian teacher, Ibrahim al-Damanhouri, they claimed he'd died because the road hadn't reached there in time.

And likewise when a jeep overturned killing the Palestinian teacher, Husam Abu Ali, people said he'd died because the road wasn't there. As for Ahmad Uthman, the Sudanese teacher who had come from the poverty of Khartoum, he said, "I shan't wait for the road to save me," and he disappeared, never to return. His voice used to travel across the sea, fresh and innocent as childhood. But the road remained the same invincible object of interest, promising candy to the children and infiltrating the leaves of the doom palm trees too, promising sweetness and joy.

Everyone bore, in his head, an idea of the aid and amenities the road would bring. They spoke of it as al-Qunfudhah's salvation; it would save the place from famine, fever and its general backwardness. With its arrival, the land would turn fertile, the mosquitoes emigrate, the wolves, foxes and snakes would disappear, and even the darkness would be modified.

But Abu Mu'id cursed the road and all those who assisted its construction, and cursed openly those who'd planned it, and imprecated against the government, silently. He was fully aware that a road coming to Sabt Shimran would have him lose his monopoly as the owner of a primitive gas station made out of a tank placed on a sand-pile, and a depression into which the car would enter in order to fill up, rather as though the vehicle was taking up a strategic military position on the front lines. Abu Mu'id could see a fleet of modern gas stations crowding the road all the way to Yemen in the south.

It took a long time for the black giant to reach the village—its color lividly pronounced against the desert. When it finally arrived at al-Sabt, Shaikh Hajar brought out a Kalashnikov, a leftover from the 1970 September war in Jordan, which had been smuggled across the desert by gun-runners, and emptied a cartridge belt into Saturn's body.

Incited by this, a movement began on the outskirts of the village and centered itself in the school yard. The animation was like that of a big wedding, and the youths jumped into the sky like winged horses and waved their canes. Others sported banners and formed a large circle around the rice which they began eating greedily after a whole day of celebrations. And when the large trays of meat were brought in, the dancers' hands were still encrusted with rice as they tore at the joints.

Abu Mu'id nudged Ahmad Lufti and asked him to hold the joint so he could tear a piece of meat from it. "That's all I'll get out of the road," he said. When the celebrants left, the *shaikh* of Sabt Shimran called a group of youths together and asked them to keep vigil on the road. He then gathered the edges of his cloak and went in search of his new young bride.

But Haj Saud was wiser. "We've never taken part in a feast at Sabt Shimran yet without the people of al-Sabt thinking we're conspiring against them," he said.

"Why Haj?"

"It's a wash-back from the old war; things were never properly resolved. Then the money came, and a new conflagration was lit."

The teachers were absent that night, all except Ahmad Lutfi; they sat in the dark in their stone rooms, lanterns extinguished, probably realizing things would never change in al-Qunfudhah, and that its parched wound would always lie open to the sky. The mosquitoes gunned around their rooms, little murderous planes fueled with pestilence. The wolves howled on the outskirts of Sabt Shimran and Thuraiban and Naqmah and al-Sawad. Only hunger ran away that night, but it didn't go far.

Ahmad Lufti alone attended the meeting. That opportunist who never let an occasion pass without exploiting it or turning it to his advantage. He was known in al-Qunfudhah for his rapacious greed, he consorted with thugs and built an empire based on mercenary terrorism. With the help of Jabir, the head of police, he converted that barren space which they called an "airport" into a bar. There was no shortage of liquor. Ahmad Lufti would journey back and forth from Namira in a private car, and in this way transport the cases of distilled wine. On his return there'd be drinking at night and the reverberation of glasses and songs.

114

Boy! Give me the glass, and the wine
Boy! Joy of my heart, give me the wine
Prepare a place for us like yesterday.
Coax the sun out of the void
and fill the glasses with its light,
and leave us drink till you can see
we only talk: in whispers.

And who can arrest the head of police?

During the first half of that year no one really spoke to him. Even those who owed him rent dispatched it through intermediaries. He cultivated his solitude and stood off like a wolf until no one in the village dared to approach him. On the evening of the road celebrations he was still alone, but he was bold to a degree that he ate his victim in front of everyone.

The wolves howled at the sky's bowl, intermittent and wild like their hunger. Perhaps it was the smell of meat on the night breeze that excited them. It was a strange night, here in this wilderness.

Ahmad Lufti slipped to Hanash's shack, knowing Hanash was far away. Lust had driven him to a state of torment. Jabir's voice kept ringing in his ears: "Why don't you let me go and do it for you?" and the words formed ever widening circles in his skull.

It didn't take him long to arrive at the shack. It lay there quiet, adjacent to the shops that awaited the souq day. Nothing stirred apart from the drum-beat of his heart. The shack comprised a wooden door and primitive straw walls.

It was one after midnight. Hanash's sister, Alya, was

asleep, soft as a fountain, dark-skinned like a lovely, peaceful night, innocent as a carnation. Ahmad Lutfi stretched out by her side. His hand played with her face, then slipped down to play with her breasts.

Was she dreaming?

When she turned over her legs went out like a wheat field. A trembling hand stretched to the top of her thighs.

Was she dreaming?

Before Alya realized what was happening, the dream had completed its cycle. She felt the weight of a body move on to her own. Something within her connected with consciousness: a dream couldn't be as heavy as that.

She screamed. Screamed. Screamed.

His hand closed over her mouth, but his body had tensed. He stared with astonishment at the rebellious body without being able to do anything.

Alya screamed again.

No one will hear you. There's nothing here but the closed shops.

She screamed again, and this time people did hear and rushed in the direction of the shack. Ahmad Lufti had disappeared. There was nothing in his place but the dark.

"Who was it?" they asked.

"Ahmad Lufti," she said.

Jabir bellowed, "Beat it! Liar!"

And when they went to Ahmad Lufti's place they found him asleep. Jabir continued to mutter, "Liar! Liar!"

They would have sentenced her were it not for the intervention of Shaikh Hajar. "Leave her, she's only a woman dreaming." He meant they should leave her to him.

It had been a long time since the smell of meat climbed

those dark mountains. All the provisions in the square had been consumed. The rice had vanished into the hungry bellies, and the bones were collected and placed in paper bags by the inhabitants of Sabt Shimran, Thuraiban, Naqmah and al-Sawad. It's a habit of which the poor are ashamed. They take the bones back to their children and re-cook them. It's a custom practiced all over the desert.

Wolves howled in the distance. It was their night too. Sabt Shimran was gathering the stones around its body. The silence was punctuated by an intermittent jungle of voices. Then like the torrential waters that rush from the heights of Aseer, they began to pour down in large packs, their eyes fixed on the lower slopes and the few lights constellating the dark. They reached the school play-ground, following their scent, and dug the earth with their paws. They nuzzled into the sand and loose surface stones searching for traces of meat. They they stopped, turned around, and as though informed by a collective dementia they turned towards the heart of the village in small packs. They leapt over walls to the courtyards of houses, digging under the doors, sniffing out the scent of bones. The sound was a familiar one to the villagers. They awoke and armed themselves with rifles or the glinting cleavers that they kept under their pillows. And as though informed of one instinct of preservation, the whole village rushed after the wolves. Old men, women, children, even the teachers who'd adopted the role of spectators set out in pursuit. The entire desert peoples united in one big scream, in one fist, in one murderous exclamation.

Ahmad Lufti stood alone at the door of his room,

leaning on stones that were still impregnated with the day's fire. No one knows who aimed the first blow, but it was the signal for sticks to rain down on him, as he too ran away like a wolf who'd strayed from the pack. By the time the wolves had reached the outskirts of the village, Ahmad Lufti was to be numbered among them, and he insinuated himself into the pack before disappearing.

The villagers chased the pack to the foot of the mountain, and then sensing their victory, they sat panting on the rocks.

Ahmad Lufti disappeared forever. Some said that the wolves ate him that night, while shepherds swore they'd seen him from time to time, a wolf, hunting with the packs of wolves.

14

"Shaikh Hajar," I said, "we need a cock."

"To kill?"

"No, we need it for our two hens."

"That's no problem," he said. "We have a cock that will suit your two hens."

"Is it a big one?"

"Yes."

"And is it tall?"

"Yes."

"How much do you want for it?"

"Money isn't a problem between us, Ustadh Muhammad," he said, but he took the proffered fifty *riyal* note with evident greed.

You still hadn't yet spoken to Aunt Jarada. If you coincided with her occasional visits to the well, you'd greet her, while she in her anxiety to get away would urge her donkey into action. It would trot in the direction of the shack, and you knew without looking at her that the anger which was in you was also written into her eyes. As for you, you were simply looking for some gesture of recognition between neighbors.

When you finally dared to approach her, she was in a state of exhaustion from the heat and the weight of the pail of water which had begun to slide back into the well after she'd succeeded in drawing it half way up the shaft. You hurried over and said, "Leave this to me, Aunt Jarada." She looked at you intently before conceding the rope to your hands, placing her back against the trunk of a large doom palm tree and falling into a deep, contemplative silence; and the mute note of pain reached you: this is the last thing I could imagine, Ghabshan!

Aunt Jarada went off without uttering a word, but not before you'd managed to say: "I wish we'd never come here, Aunt Jarada, we'd have spared you this fatigue!"

The next day at noon her answer came:

"Son, it's not your fault. You're not to blame."

You carried the two water containers for her, and secured them on the donkey's back.

She said, "God bless you, son!" in the way that a mother would. At the time you didn't realize why both of the hens proved incapable of laying a single egg. In this climate eggs arrived from Jeddah containing embryos. Everything turned putrid. When Ustadh Muhammad opened the glass bowl in which he'd put a pound of white cheese, only yesterday, it had turned green and black with putrescent patches. The sun wasn't even up when he examined it and found it was rotten.

"We bought it yesterday," he said, "only yesterday, and look at it." From between two half-closed eyes, you said, "This means the temperature here's too high."

Your answer failed to convince Ustadh Muhammad. He stepped towards the door and threw the container and its contents as far as his anger could reach. You heard the shattering of glass as the container exploded on impact with stone.

Ustadh Muhammad breathed deeply, as though he'd freed himself of all the rottenness on the surface of the earth, and stretched out on his bed.

"Are you rested now?" I asked.

He didn't answer. He looked at you and then went out.

Two days later you began dreaming about seeing fresh food. When you suggested buying two hens he didn't oppose the idea. But then you needed a cock. And here it was, strutting around in the room like a little tiger.

You said, "I used to think hens didn't lay eggs without a cock, but these are barren even with the male bird here."

But Aunt Jarada's voice crossed the flaming distance one day, "Ustadh Muhammad, your hen's laid an egg in my shack."

"And where's the egg?" you asked.

"Here it is," she said, and you thanked her.

"We won't eat it," you said to Ustadh Muhammad. "We'll keep it as a souvenir."

Ustadh Muhammad laughed sarcastically and asked, "And why doesn't our hen lay its eggs in our house? Haven't you seen our cock's wounds? It's Aunt Jarada's doing," he said, "after the two cocks had fought our hens became the victor's protegées."

121

Hearing this you realized you'd have to keep your cock away from the house for a week to make it forget its defeat and recover its initial virility. It needed to reassert its dominance, otherwise it would remain impotent for the rest of its life.

"We'll send it to Amara," you said.

You brought it back after a week. The two cocks fought again, with the same result.

"Aunt Jarada," you said, "would you sell us your cock?"

She said, "How's that, Ustadh, what about my hens?"

I said, "Our cock should be sufficient."

Aunt Jarada laughed until the tears streamed from her eyes. "But yours isn't fit, Ustadh, it's not up to it." And punctually every noon, Aunt Jarada would call, "Ustadh Muhammad!"

You'd come out, or Ustadh Muhammad would, and immediately the warm egg would be in your hand. But that didn't last long. Aunt Jarada's red cock came to rout your two hens from the room. It was a small cock, and in terms of size no match for your own, which only served to fuel your anger. You decided to lay a trap for it by strewing corn on the floor and closing the door behind it once it began to feed. When you closed one of the two windows it sensed something was wrong. It made for the eastern window, which you'd already closed. You chased it from one corner to another until at last it settled, defeated, between your hands. Beaten, but still rebellious.

You tied it to one of the bed posts, and opened the door. It took a long time for your defeated cock to enter the room, and no sooner did he catch sight of his aggressor than he retreated, then advanced cautiously, evincing fear. Only when assured of the incapacity of its adversary to move, did it make a positive attack. The two fought in a bloody foam and the contest was decided by ropes and not the challenge of strength. Aunt Jarada's cock looked for a place of retreat away from the enraged beak and claws that had sensed an easy victory.

After the result had been decided, you calmly untied Aunt Jarada's cock. It walked away with heavy, dragging steps, blood covering its neck, face and wings, while your cock followed it.

"Ustadh Muhammad," a voice called. You let her call again before coming out with a wrap around your waist.

"What is it, Aunt Jarada?"

"Your cock wounded ours, Ustadh."

"Two cocks fought together," you said. "That's all!"

Two days later she asked you to buy the cock for the sum of twenty-five *riyals*, to which you gladly assented. You knew this was bound to happen, for the inhabitants here find constant cock-fighting an ill-omen. But Aunt Jarada's pessimism was greater than you expected.

That night you ate hard meat which the fire couldn't cook. "Are you rested now?" Ustadh Muhammad asked. "Yes," you said. "From now on we can eat fresh eggs." But the two hens, the brown and the white, continued to lay their eggs in Aunt Jarada's shack. Every few days Aunt Jarada would own up and say, "The egg's yours," and then the days grew to be weeks and multiplied to months, and finally she said nothing at all.

15

The feeling grew. You discovered that there was someone who obsessed you even more than Ustadh Muhammad, and that person was Fatima. You needed nothing to remind you of her, she who'd cut across the noon like a sun-shaft in that space between the police precinct and the Emir's headquarters.

It was as if the cumulative fatigue and destruction the days had brought, together with the sense of estrangement and dissociation weren't enough. The sudden meeting deprived you of words, it cut you off from self-analysis as to what was happening around you, inside you. A woman dressed in a black cloak in the middle of the desert, surrounded by sand on every side, and still wrapping the cloak tightly around her. You searched for your own body but couldn't find it. There was only Fatima. Or was it really her? You felt a crucial relationship existed between the two of you, an inscrutable relationship, one that had crystallized in the osmotic fluids of dream and externalized itself into a reality.

You began to question whether this was Fatima of whom Ustadh Muhammad had spoken, or Abu Muhammad's daughter? You grew confused and shouted out "Fatima" and rushed after her, but she refused to look back. You caught up with her and shook her by the shoulders; you didn't let go until the cloak had slipped from her head and shoulders.

"Fatima!"

She stared at your face, trying to suppress the tears welling inside her, one of which escaped with the same import as though the globe had fallen and spun into the void.

For a single moment that was extended to a lifetime you both entered into a state of timelessness, presence that was absence, disembodiment that was air.

She bent down, and still bare-headed and looking lost, gathered up her cloak. Her dusky skin and austere silence covered the earth, brushed it like a pair of corpses that must be removed from the cycle of life. Fatima went off, her cloak beating the ground like a black flag. A small room awaited her dry shriveled body.

Suddenly you grew alert. You shook . . . as if waking up to find yourself between the millstones of a huge mill.

You didn't dare look around you. "Is there anyone there?"

"No one," she said.

When you looked there was no Fatima.

You looked and you weren't you.

125

. . . .

. . . .

That morning Ustadh Muhammad came.

"What morning?"

"I don't know."

That morning, but it wasn't exactly morning, it was noon.

That noon.

"What noon?"

"I don't know."

That noon, but it wasn't exactly noon . . . it was evening.

"What evening?"

"I don't know."

"That evening, but it wasn't exactly evening . . . that . . ."

"I don't know."

Ustadh Muhammad came and fluttered on the door of the room. He beat it with his wings. I got up and opened and looked out at the empty space. There was no reason for all this joy.

He circled twice around the room, then soared up high. He beat the air with his broad chest and his shining wing feathers, infusing me with his own enthusiasm. The bats had been absent for more than a week from the room's dark center.

"A whole week without bats!"

"What could have happened?" you asked.

"I don't know," he replied.

"We're going crazy," I said, "let's speak in a more sensible language."

"Fatima!" he said.

126

"It's too confusing."

"Abu Muhammad's daughter," he exclaimed.

There's more than one Abu Muhammad in these villages, so I said nothing. We agreed to terminate the conversation.

"You must be fairer," I said, "and share my grief and joy with me."

"I'll share your joy," he confessed.

That day, but it wasn't exactly a day, he spoke of many things.

"What makes you happy?" I asked.

He said, "I didn't talk to her about anything, but I felt she agrees with me. It's a profound experience. This is the first time it has happened to me."

"That's insulting," I said.

"No, there are people who understand you better than you understand yourself."

"All right, then, it's not insulting. What happened?"

That day, which was too peculiar to be a day, was his time of confession. And there in that uncomfortable spot between the police precinct and the Emir's palace, a place which gathers the desert peoples, the Sabt souq spread. Abu Muhammad went from one vegetable box to another, staring at the oranges which were beginning to grow warm in the sun. His hand went out, tired, tentative, its veins protruding through the skin, and he touched the bright little suns. He withdrew it wounded.

"They may be from there . . . they may be from there!"

Abu Muhammad shook his head and said nothing. When he looked up our eyes collided. There was a momentary flicker of embarrassment on my part before we collected ourselves in the manner of two people

127

who've concluded a long dialogue agreeably. We moved off in silent harmony, something that remained unbroken until we reached the door of a small room.

"Fatima!" he called.

The door opened with the contained whirlwind of a woman who hasn't left her cave for a thousand years. But inside, all was calm, the trees were regaining their greenness.

It was unknown for a man to allow a bachelor to enter his house if it had a young woman in it. This was the law of the desert. Abu Muhammad, however, turned around and began the noon prayer. And it was strange, we found ourselves talking in a silent language. The necessity for raw words had disappeared.

I felt a great need for a branch to support me, or a frame that could contain me and protect me from disintegrating. That branch could have been you, or it could have been Abu Muhammad.

Fatima brought the tea in, and this simple act put us at ease. I looked into her benevolent face that showed, too, signs of bitter torment. I screamed, "This is me!"

Abu Muhammad looked at you, smiled, then laughed until the earth turned green. I left that small room silently. Three dull words had served to fracture the friendly atmosphere.

I tried to imagine Fatima getting me out of there. The world was like a dark well or a cage. And perhaps she wondered, "Could this stranger get me out of here?" You nursed the illusion of two birds in a cage, searching for freedom, each in the other.

That morning although it couldn't really be described as morning, I said, "Boy, these are just dreams."

"You were born ignorant," he said.

"But you don't understand. It was only that I felt there

was someone who understood me without the necessity of speech, and whom I understood in the same way. That person could have been you."

"It could have been," he added. "But I'm tired of expending my days on this nonsense."

"I had no need to meet Fatima again. In this vast narrow desert, saturated with oil and tuberculosis, I was looking for you both, but I found her before I found you. But here we are, two birds in a cage looking for freedom, each in the other."

"So?"

"It feels like there's a live ember in my head, I'm not well."

Ustadh Muhammad looked for an exit. It was as if time had come to an end and the sun was coming down until it touched the earth. The bats circled round and round the room, and floods poured down the mountain slopes carrying everything before them.

"It was a dream," you said.

"You're not capable of dreaming any more" he replied. "You wouldn't know what a dream is."

"And did you have to keep on colliding with walls in order to wake up?"

"No," he said. "Living with you did that."

When I suggested he leave, he hesitated at first, then got up and walked out. Fatima dropped the tea tray. The glass shattered into glinting shards and splinters. It was difficult to retrieve from the surface of sand.

"I'm broken," Ustadh Muhammad screamed. Abu Muhammad returned and opened the door.

"What's happened?" he asked.

"Nothing, nothing, Father." She knelt on the ground

and with bleeding fingers retrieved the jagged splinters.
And in the parcel of land between the police precinct and
the Emir's house, Abu Muhammad was beating the sand
with his feet, while the noonday sun remorselessly drum-
med on his head.

It would arrive
I'm not sure from where,
come here and tap
on the cracked wood.
I'd call to it,
bird, be my heart
and my consciousness
and go to the end of time
the harvest of places
        and people
then return
and tell my blood
that these steps were not the beginning
        of my death.
It would come
from an unknown source,
sure of its place,
and once they surprised it perched
on the branch of my heart.
It was small,
small
small.
And when they caught it by the wings
I cried:
—a wound in my soul—
"Let me fly away."

130

16

Now it's the night again. Many creatures wait for that dark, to find their savage nature again, and Fatima looks to it in order to enter into a union with the infinite. She would transcend the misery of her condition and enter that youthful presence, leaving destruction behind.

This was Sabt Shimran.

The feverish lung of the desert, the hungry birds of blood.

This was Sabt Shimran.

An open gate to nothing, a tubercular bacillus, a fistful of sand that filters over the emaciated body.

> A mud forest
> with granite trees.

Fires of memory
fingers of stone.

A horrific time. She who stood between the butterfly of
dream and the fire of reality, asked you one day: "Why
are you so like a child?"

"Because I don't ask the garden forgiveness when I
pick a flower."

I don't apologize to the earth when I run on its face.
Nor do I apologize to the sun when I cross it.

She might have smiled at your eloquence, and forgotten her walls, and the savage passage of time that moved
across her features. She might have gone on smiling until
stars dropped out of the sky, light opened windows and
streamed into fountains, and young girls let down their
braids.

The rose that had grown out of the praries of fever,
sprung up like a red moon to crown her, and then broke
her heart.

You said, "Fatima, do you realize you've been here for
two years? Why?"

Her small breasts quivered. She withdrew as though
staring into the mental fissure you'd opened.

"Why, Fatima?"

The question surprised her, and she made no attempt
to answer. Her body shook, while she gathered herself to
face the naked truth.

"Fatima, the sea's blue. Doesn't that tempt you? And
the sky is blue. Doesn't that tempt you? Let's run to the
sea and cross it, and center our vision in the sky." But the

young girl adorned by the gardens grew confused, trying
to distinguish dream from reality.

> The little girl said
> to the bird of the waves, "I'm your wing,"
> and to the shadow of the chained place
> "I'm your wing,"
> to the color of the sky
> to the song of water
> "I'm your wing."
> She said,
>   and said,
> but when pain overtook
> in the noonday fire,
> she fell back bloodied
> before she refound the echo
> or was able to fly.

What window illuminated by the sun has been smashed in
you? What hammer has broken your ribs, so that you live
joyless in the dark of pain.

"I'm tired, Fatima. I'm a bird who chose to sing of life
not death."

"I can't distinguish whether you are an illusion or
reality. It's as if you were like them."

"How?" I asked.

"I can't endure the touch of rough hands, or the touch
of soft hands. I'm squeezed between the hedgehog and
the snake. I read once that what money I possess should
liberate me, whereas now my hand's weighed down. I
remember that good man, my father, saying once that a
free woman would rather starve than sell her body—but

he ate from the price of my body."

"Here in the desert," I said, "femininity and masculinity disappear; it's as if we were one sex."

The sun wheeled above the streets of Sabt Shimran, searching out the few remaining fortresses. Bullets no longer whine through the air, but there is still a war enacted between the mountain summit and the slope, between hunger and corncobs, between water and tuberculosis, between one tribe and another, between money and the amenities it should bring.

Fatima, unused to your absence, flung open the door and sat in the entrance, waiting.

She, who showed such caution, waited, then broke her silence and said:

"Father, Ustadh Muhammad no longer visits us."

All she needed to be able to ask him was some audacity. That money which never gave her freedom should give her at least some audacity.

"Maybe he has the fever, Fatima."

It may be the fever.

"Fatima, it's night. The wolves are abroad with their burning eyes. Go into the house."

Fatima huddled in the dark corner of her room away from the light. She looked around the room without moving her head. Then abruptly, she stood up, and tried to reach the window. It was too high for her as she strained upwards—it was like an inaccessible prison window. She almost forced her head off her shoulders in the effort, and her toes almost pushed the globe into the void.

Ustadh Muhammad had become a part of the dark. Out there in the night, the stones crawled, the cactus trees moved forward. The sky fell down to the earth. The

134

hands that plunged into her soft flesh went in deep and stayed there.

"Do you know what it means to live here?"

. . . . !

From the moment I first arrived in Jeddah, I realized everything. There's no place here for dream or reality; it's fever that dominates. It harvests the spirit. It lives in the dry tree and the corn fields, it inhabits the water and the air. And fever here is one's absence, not the bite of a mosquito. Nor does the problem lie with al-Qunfudhah; even the most modern city would be plague-ridden in this desert. One place is much like any other, fever operates on a level of dissociation. It drives you to the edge of the world, to a concourse with wolves and jackals. It's as though al-Qunfudhah is the shot that pierced your slumber. The dream seemed so real, so concrete.

The next evening when your absence inhabited her own vacuum, the earth seemed too narrow for her steps. She slipped away with her black hair let down like a horse's mane, slunk off in her white nightgown, her lips trembling, her face expressive of fatigue, until she reached the door. She could endure it no longer.

"Where are you going Fatima?"

The voice surprised her, it was sharp and harsh. No sooner did it strike her consciousness than the stone room opened to the world.

Run. She screamed as if she were driving a herd of horses that had become frozen by death. Run . . . You must see the world, and your hair must cover all the mountains of the earth. At the beginning she tripped over the edge of her nightgown, pain consuming her.

Run, Fatima!

"Stop!" Abu Muhammad shouted, and the house-windows shook.

Run!

She ran, covering the distance between the souq and the Emir's house. Her shadow pursued her.

"Where's Thuraiban?" she shouted.

"Down there in the south."

"But he came from there."

"It's over there in the east."

"But he came from there."

"It's over there in the west."

"But he came from there."

"It's over there in the north."

"But he came from there."

What other directions are there to pursue? Run, Fatima! As she ran, the earth moved under her feet and panted with her. She reached the foot of the mountain, its towering black contour absorbed by the night. Climb! She ascended the slopes like one scaling the heart of darkness. Each time she fell over she had to start all over again. Her father's shouts had multiplied into an echo-chamber of effects that bounced back from the summits, the sharp ridges, and slapped her in the face. It was as though her pursuers were in front of her. She stopped short, confused, and was about to run back in the direction she had come from. Hundreds of flashlights now mixed with the eyes of foxes and wolves. Hundreds of people.

Blood spurted from her fingers as she pushed her nails into the stubborn granite walls of the night. The stars were beginning to fall.

Run, Fatima!

As she ran, the lights closed in on her, yellow and red

fluctuating beams. If she could she would have built a wall of darkness between herself and her adversaries. But they moved in nearer, faces spinning like whirlpools, her father's, Jabir's, Abu Abd al-Rahman's, and those of the school attendants. All of them stared at her in silence.

Her eyes burnt, terror flapped out on the surface of her skin. They had caught up with her just before dawn. They brought her back in her white nightgown, that symbol of her arrested flight.

17

When they brought her back captive
she was no longer Fatima.
She spread through the mountains
a star, a question.
She washed the shadows
of those who rested
after their hatred,
and from the veins in her hands
you sprang out alive.

It was terrifying; it was savage, full of insidious death.
The village narrowed in, the lights diminished. Vul-
tures crowded the sky; pain lived between embers of fever
and the freezing of extremities. Her life contracted to a
crystal set in stone walls. No one thought of crossing the

threshold. Instead they watched, and those who saw Fatima in her white nightgown swore they'd seen her quite naked.

"Madness hit her brain," someone said. "No," another said, "her father caught her going to meet one of the school teachers, and she'd no option but flight."

"If I'd caught her naked, I would have stripped her of her skin, too."

"Teachers are no different when it comes to a woman's honor."

"You! You should keep silent. What do you know of honor?"

"I don't know, you canine?! You're one of those who try to forget doing ablutions before they go to prayer!"

"That's none of your business."

"Go away, before I'm tempted to use this blade to silence you."

"Come on, you're friends! You're brothers!"

The sun held off. The square near the mosque darkened; the rest of the day resembled the night.

Soon the village began dragging its children again, cowering from the sun's intensity which focuses its heat-spot on the nape. Abu Muhammad huddled in the eastern corner of his room, pressing his feverish hands to his knees. And Fatima huddled in the opposite corner, a broken gazelle, devoid of all animation.

Four bewildered eyes, a blackish-green stove, two disheveled beds, a kettle, scattered tea cups, a sandy floor, a door, a well-locked door.

Neither of them dared to make the simplest move or turn their head. There was time enough to listen to one's heart beat and tame the disturbing contents of one's memory.

139

Outside, the spot of light moved, it climbed the wall and tried to make access through the almost unattainable.

"Can the sun suffer from vertigo, father?"

Its rays had begun to mount an upright stone block and establish a focal-point in the center. How long would it take before that concentrated energy split the stone and traveled back to its home behind the mountains?

The door stayed shut all day. Fatima didn't go to school, nor did Abu Muhammad perform his noon and afternoon prayers in the mosque, as was his custom. "Shall I knock on their door, Abu Abd al-Rahman?"

"Let them be. What happened yesterday has never been heard of before in the village. A woman dressed only in a white nightgown, leaving her room bare-foot in the middle of the night. If we hadn't reached her in time the hyenas would have eaten her, or a snake poisoned her. Let them be, Um Abd al-Rahman."

Abu Abd al-Rahman left his courtyard, fondling his white beard and scrutinizing the sky with his eyes.

A woman in a white nightgown, bare-foot in the middle of the night . . . Nothing like this had ever happened before. And he disappeared.

Um Abd al-Rahman waited. Her eyes never left the wooden door. When darkness fell she looked to see whether light would show through cracks in the door. In the end she couldn't wait, so decided to knock at the door.

"Abu Muhammad . . . Fatima . . . Fatima . . ."

At first her voice was timid, afraid of scratching the tragic silence that enveloped the place. She knocked at the door a second, a third time. When Abu Abd al-Rahman returned, she confronted him saying:

140

"Don't tell me they've lost the impetus to speak."

> My star is broken
> my hand is bloodied
> my step has exploded
> I stare into
> A chasm
> A chasm

Fatima shivered. She stared at the ceiling as though half expecting it to cave in. She heard someone knocking at the door, and once again was fixed into the nightmare of running. She came out of her corner, eyes staring, her mind full of terror. Distraction had numbed her sense of feeling.

"Fatima."

And Fatima kept crawling away from the wall, as if the knocks were coming out of the heart of stones to attack her. Suddenly she collided with a body. She'd reached the opposite corner of the room. She screamed, as though surprised there was a living person sharing her room.

Abu Muhammad shook when he heard the scream. His fingers stretched, trying to feel the voice, trembling. At the other edge of the night a body was creeping away, returning to its corner.

At first she imagined it was someone else. It couldn't have been Muhammad, he who first came to her from the corners of the souq. For a moment she was convinced he was now climbing the other mountain slope. "The other mountain slope?" Then it was coming back to her. Her flight seemed remote now, something closer to a nightmare.

It had begun that day when he came to you, or when he shook your shoulders and your cloak slipped down. Was it possible too that fever had consumed him, or that he was climbing the other slope of the mountain? Or perhaps they'd brought him back with their brutal hands, after joining with the wolves in chasing him. He may be there . . . there.

There was still some life left in the memory of two birds in a cage, each searching for its freedom in the other.

She was so alone she couldn't even bring herself to shout "Father!"

That morning her father returned unusually early. He said nothing, not even under the provocation of her questioning. "What are you concealing from me, father?" she asked.

In the end he gave in and spoke. "It's impossible, trying to turn this sand into earth."

"It's the problem of the land, then!"

The scorching winds have burnt the crops again. The buds were blown off.

"It's this everlasting wind, Fatima, which has prevented the desert from preserving a single flower for hundreds of years. It's the wind's raid. But I'll never give up, droughts never stopped me going on. I'll go back and begin again."

He'd gone before she had time to speak. He went straight to Abu Abd al-Rahman's and knocked on the door.

"I need the ox."

"Now?"

"Yes, right now!"

Um Abd al-Rahman, sunk into the gray years of her forties, backed away. But the ox, which sat heavily ruminating its dry corn leaves, wouldn't budge. Abu Muhammad rebuked it, nudged it, but the creature wouldn't move. It continued to stare off and ignore his presence.

"You'll kill the ox, Abu Muhammad!"

"It's he who'll be the death of me!"

Abu Muhammad held on to the ox by its horns, almost turning the creature over, before it stood up, lazily. The ox ambled to the door and looked up at the sky, then pushed its head through in order to see the world more clearly. It looked to both sides and then went back inside.

Abu Muhammad nudged it, while the ox turned round and stared at the face drenched with sweat, disappointment and determination, before heading off towards the field through burning sands.

Um Abd al-Rahman went back and knocked on the door again. Fatima whispered, "How long will this go on father?"

The noon was suffocating. She repeated her question with each renewed knock at the door, that enquiry to which she knew he had no answer. "Will you keep on until the cities run away from your footsteps, and until you've created your own death in life?"

She knew these questions coming from her small mouth were impossible to answer. Her eyes were full of fever and estrangement, and her fingertips found release in that enquiry from scratching the stone walls.

"How long will you go on, father?"

Abu Muhammad shifted his feet firmly on the sand. He opened the door, revealing his presence as a tired old man with a white beard and a *kufiyya* chaotically settled on

143

his head. Abu Muhammad heard her repeat the question again. He was crossing the road to the house of a prince. Everything ended and began here.

"We're going back, Fatima," he said. "Everything will end today."

A soft hand kneaded her breast, followed by a rougher, more urgent one. The hands multiplied. It was only Um Abd al-Rahman's hand that was patting her face and hair.

Her questions grew more intense, until her crowded skull emptied itself of her enquiries. Had it been listening the entire globe might have heard her momentary scream. Then she exploded, her delirium shook the house, ran its walls to the four quarters. Her hands, her fingers, her little skull, her chestnut hair, her feet, her twenty-two years, her shadow, everything detonated and scattered. Pieces flew up in the air, then came back slowly in the direction of the earth. They hung over the airport, the blackened houses and the crows which were alighting at that moment on the baked walls of the cemetery. People carried on walking around as if nothing had happened, while Fatima's parts spread out over the stones and flaming sands. She exploded with the impact of dynamite.

A crow saw a human larynx fall out of the sky, still hoarding a suffocated scream. The throat plummeted down near to it. The crow shivered and tried to fly away, but its wings had become locked. It closed its eyes and attempted to move and finally beat into a ragged flight.

Abu Muhammad had left the Emir's house, screaming. It was an end. He'd go down to al-Qunfhudhah to get his passport, then he'd leave these sands. But he was too late.

18

In these days and seasons which undifferentiatedly intermesh one with the other, united by a thread of flame, and in the chaos induced by self-disintegration and dissociation, your search was for a reality that would let your feet tread the ground, or a dream that projected beyond the continuous nightmare.

What you knew for sure was that he'd gone. It was his means of going which remained inexplicable. Did he go clean through the wall or the door or through the little vent by which the bats entered the room? Or was he still here?

You stared at all the things in the room, but forgot to stare at yourself. You searched the summits, the plains, and poked among the dismembered camels washed down by the floods. You went off into the wilderness as Saad's daughter had done, and watched hawks soar in the thermals. And you wished you had their infallibly sharp eyes, the levity of their wings.

You shouted at the horizon until your voice reverberated with thunder. You dug into the earth, where once a subterranean stream had flowed, but there was no one. Neither the principal of the school, nor Jabir the head of police asked after him. Haj Saud eyed you suspiciously, and intimated you should see a doctor—these corresponding identities seemed implausible: the color of the eyes, of the skin, the height, the hair, the memories.

But they returned on their motorcycles, took their thousand *riyals*, and the story repeats itself. They arrive whenever one of the expatriate teachers dies, and knock on the door. They usually come at night, for they've motored across the enormity of the desert, explosive space peopled by wolves, bats, hungry greenfinches and crows, and inexorable white ants.

Your tired eyes watched the movement of the darkness, or was it the light within the dark? Inscrutable, textured moving minutes of black in which you drown. You were searching for a point of clarity, something which was luminous without being light, something associated with the day but not the sun. You pulled the cover tightly over your body, your head protruding from the blanket. There was life in your eyes, embers of blood shone in your forehead, and a sea flowed under your clothes, small, undulant waves after the big storms which had charged your cells, broken your bones.

You remembered Fatima and were almost convinced that you'd known her somewhere else, in another time, and that the cloak which slipped from her head and shoulders was nothing else but the long night that stands between you and her. She may be the night. With a trembling hand you tried to make of the dark a tangible thing, only your hands returned freezing, empty.

"Fatima!" you called, and your voice reverberated in fragmented sound-waves. The night never ends; cock-crow alone begins to lift the curtain of night from your eyes.

You'd wept, you'd almost given up hope—you'd searched widely for him, and your only illogical explanation was that the earth had swallowed him. When you stretched out on his bed it seemed to you that you used to sleep there, closer to the north window where the air blows cool at night, and the heat furnaces during the day.

After searching through his clothes for the thousand *riyals*, you decided to try them on for size. His wardrobe consisted of three shirts and two pairs of pants, with an additional shirt and pair of pants hung up on a green braided plastic rope. They fitted you perfectly, so you decided to wear them. We could have been one person, you thought, your anger rising again at the lack of interest shown by the principal and Haj Saud in his disappearance. Then you'd tremble thinking, "What if I were Ustadh Muhammad himself?" It was impossible to rationalize why Jabir, the chief of police, had chosen to overlook the matter. He came one evening, then never returned. Since then, the interval of time had risen like a wall to the sky. You could no longer find a coherence in things, nor a meaning in those black sails traveling towards primordial caves.

How you wished for Fatima's presence, or that the silence could reveal a single word that would restore fertility to the sands. She alone would have understood your predicament and found an answer to the questions.

"On that morning."

"Which morning?"

"I don't know."

"On that morning, but it wasn't exactly morning, it was noon."

"At that noon."

"Which noon?"

"I don't know."

"That noon, but now I think of it, it was evening."

"On that evening."

"Which evening?"

"I don't know."

"On that. . ."

You stood at her door, and with a trembling hand pressed her fingers. You needed nothing more to open a window of light in your heart. And suddenly, everything exploded, the fingers, the body's salt reserves, the floods of live embers. And you were alone again.

And Ustadh Muhammad? Ustadh Muhammad, was he really here in this room, lying between the dirt floor and the cracked ceiling, exactly three yards away? I gave him everything I had, and yet I couldn't keep him there. He could have been screaming somewhere, his voice pitched to an insane hoarseness.

Salim al-Shimrani aimed at the two birds. They were on the topmost branch of the tree. In the heat of the noon, their delicate beaks sought communion. Each had a black ring under the neck and a yellow dot under the tail. The shot was like an absurd game that sundered their communion. A red blotch appeared on one of the breasts, a drop of blood, and a bird falling out of the tree. Was it the male or the female?

A violent clapping of wings succeeded the shot as the other bird wheeled up and then returned to the branch with its minute blood-stain, and the presence of death that formed a trajectory rising to the slopes of the Hijaz mountains. Salim al-Shimrani looked around him, desperate to find something to protect him from the beating of wings and this outraged voice. He realized the rifle was still in his hand. The surviving bird kept alighting every other minute on a branch that almost touched the ground, without taking its eyes off the tiny corpse.

Salim knew he must shoot or the little bird would pursue him across the face of the earth. It fell, bloodied; but Salim went far away, not daring to retrieve the two tiny bodies.

You can no longer anticipate from which direction the bullet will come to you. Scorching blood flows from the walls, fountains from the sand, burns out of the silence and the night. The darkness is red, bloody; the fingers reaching for the light, the protruding eyes, the innumerable questions. You lack wings on which to climb into the sky, and a song that is composed more of life than of death. Your friend is on an endless road; he disappears each time you catch sight of him. He's only visible when you stop looking. You wade in his blood without seeing him—he's always one step ahead of you.

Was I mad to a degree that Jabir never returned, and the principal was content with his usual daily silence and dictation mistakes, and his involvement in the Sabt souq and writing letters to the Department of Education?

Everything around you's calm, and the familiar voice

reaches you. You grip the bedcovers, but the voice approaches. It's possible of course that fever still burns in your blood.

No!

Now the voice grows louder. It climbs the hill. There's no escape from it. The ground won't open, nor will the ceiling. The roaring stops. The rhythm of footsteps pronounces itself in the sandy courtyard, succeeded by knocks at the door. And like an old horse attacked by wolves from every side you turned around on yourself. You looked for a space, any space which could conceal your thin body, but to no avail. The voice came at you from everywhere. Hide, it said, for the big winds have returned. And after the echo had dispersed there were renewed explosions—each one more terrifying. The doors and the walls shook; the night sky rocked. There's no escape.

"Who is it?"

"It's us," they answered.

Your hand reached for the flashlight, and the eye of light opened. It moved over the plates and the cooking pot, and stopped at the door. The knocking had abated. You were about to return to bed, when the hammering started all over again.

You opened the door.

There were five of them. The flashlight shifted its focal spot. It highlighted a face that you rushed to embrace.

"So you've come back at last! I always knew you would, I was convinced of it."

He freed his body from your arms.

"Who'd return, you madman?" he said.

"You. You're Ustadh Muhammad."

"Ustadh Muhammad doesn't exist, there's no one but you here."

You stared at the faces which surrounded your central focus.

"Where did you find him?" you asked.

"This man isn't Ustadh Muhammad," they said.

You threw the light at their faces. "But it is h. . . ."

The word froze on your lips, your throat was suddenly dry. You rushed towards one of them.

"It's you, you're Ustadh Muhammad," you shouted.

"No, you are," he said.

You thought for a moment the characters were illusory—mirror-people who were unreal and only reflected what they saw. There was the hair, the eyes, the body-height, the fatigue mapped out in their features. You were terrified.

"We've prepared everything," they said, "the money, the coffin, all we lack is your corpse."

"My corpse?"

"Let's conclude this business," they said.

You were about to protest you weren't Ustadh Muhammad, but you swallowed the sentence at the last moment.

"But I'm not dead!" you appealed.

"That's what you always say. Didn't you beg us to come back when we left you the first time."

"How did you know?"

They didn't answer.

"Didn't you pay a thousand *riyals* towards the cost of your own burial?"

"I paid the money in the hope you wouldn't return."

"And having paid, don't you see that you're actually

dead. What does it matter to you if we took your body?"

"But I'm not dead."

"We told you, you keep on making that mistake."

They closed in on you, averting the flashlight with their hands. You looked towards the desert that invited you to escape through the wide open spaces. The two hens and the cock came down to search for their daily food.

They abandoned their motorcycles and pursued you. Five black shadows directed towards your body that was burning with fever. You tripped over something that resembled you.

A lock of hair.

A braid.

A hand.

A throat.

And in the middle of the square Abu Muhammad had been revolving around his daughter's corpse since yesterday noon, his hands trembling, his look fixed, while the village went in the direction of the roads and the stony pastures, without seeing anything.

You took hold of him, and shook him: "Abu Muhammad, where's Fatima?" He pointed to the earth and continued moving in a circle.

Death became clear to you in a moment of blinding clarity. When you looked behind you, they were running. The sun showed above the summits of the Hijaz mountains, vague, indistinct, barely illuminating the village.

Mirrors, mirrors, mirrors.

This isn't Sabt Shimran, but a forest of mirrors. Are there other teachers crossing the street, at this dead hour, or are you alone?

Mirrors, mirrors, mirrors.

You ran up to one of them. You took hold of him.

"Here you are at last, you've come back," you said.

He removed your hand from his shoulder, and went on his way.

You ran in the direction of another who was coming from the dirt square of the souq.

"Here you are at last," you said, "you've come back."

"Are you mad, Ustadh Muhammad? Who's come back?"

"Who's come back? You or I?"

He left.

"None of you exist," you shouted. "None of you."

The five were now indistinguishable from the mob of similar faces that crowded in. The crowd watched you silently. You took hold of Abu Muhammad's hand and screamed, "Go to al-Qunfudhah. Take your passport and run for the coast. You're free to do that now."

"And you?" Abu Muhammad asked, like one waking from a long trance.

I said, "They'll say, go to hell, you can't leave before the year's out."

Your eyes moved in a terrified fashion. The second shot was ready. It was necessary to run or drop. Jabir approached from the village with long strides.

"Get out of here, Abu Muhammad," you said.

"We'll go together," he said.

He held you. You broke loose from his embrace, and ran in the direction of the sea. You couldn't understand how the distance between the Hijaz mountains and the coast had grown so huge and yet so small. You collided with the waves and turned back. You tore through black stones, and the wolves and foxes ran away, the monkeys screamed, blood came streaming out. Then you headed back to the sea like a frightened horse trying to jump a high fence.

Abu Muhammad rushed after you and ran at your side. On the other side of the dunes, the waves came into view, a line of surf breaking your flight.

You both turned back towards the mountains, then once again made for the sea. The sun was climbing the sky, the mountains grew more distinct, the sea dashed on the foreshore. Blood was streaming from veins. Then the sea fixed you with its eye, and a gray wave opened, backed by the wind. It raised the edges of Abu Muhammad's *kufiyya*, and sent your hair loose on the surface of the water, streaming out into the current.

You looked behind you. The five were returning towards Thuraiban, dragging one of the teachers with them. He looked like you, almost identical, so that you couldn't know if it was really you, or another, or even one of them.

THE END

About the Translators

MAY JAYYUSI was born in Amman, Jordan to Palestinian parents, and was educated at London University and Boston University. She is a PROTA reader and translator, and has worked extensively in the process of selection of the poetry and fiction translated by PROTA. Aside from her work on PROTA's four anthologies of Arabic fiction and poetry, she has translated Ghassan Kanafani's *All That's Left to You and Other Stories* (1990), and Zayd Mutee' Dammaj's novel *Your Hostage*. She has also translated a collection of the poetry of Muhammad al-Maghut, *The Fan of Swords* (1991) and is presently working on the translation of Yahya Yakhlif's novel *The Lake*. She lives with her husband and two children in Jerusalem.

JEREMY REED is the acclaimed author of *By the Fisheries* which received the Somerset Maugham Award in 1985. His many books of poetry include *Selected Poems* and *Nineties*. He is also author of three novels: *The Lipstick Boys*, *Blue Rock* and *Red Eclipse*. Born in Jersey in the Channel Islands, he now lives in London.